Trail Toward Destiny

Phyllis B. Godwin

Copyright © 1997 Phyllis Booth-Godwin

All rights reserved.

ISBN: 9798390879429

DEDICATION

Forty-three years ago, GOD changed me from a Church member to a Born-Again child of His own. Thank You, LORD, for waiting for me.
Now is the day of Salvation 2 Corinthians 6:2

CONTENTS

Chapter		Page
1	A New Life	1
2	The Journey Begins	26
3	Breakfast in Erie	40
4	A Sister and a Hat	51
5	Welcome to Marshall!	64
6	The Wagon Master	73
7	A Dinner Invitation	87
8	An Unexpected Proposal	99
9	A Wagon, An Oxen Team, and Engagement Ring	110
10	Peterson Party Planners	127
11	The Quilting	136
12	Children for Rachel	150
13	Sisters to the Rescue	160
14	Mr. Wheelers Rules	172
15	Stepping Out in Faith	184

This is an inspirational work of fiction in the form of an autobiography. Any resemblance to persons living or dead is coincidental. President Lincoln signed the Homestead Act on May 20, 1862. It remained active for 124 years until it was repealed in 1976 (History.com)

ACKNOWLEDGMENTS

Thank you, Harry. Without your love and support, none of this would be possible.

One
A New Life

Come unto me, all ye that labour and are heavy laden, and I will give you rest. Matthew 11:28

At the moment of my greatly anticipated birth, I claimed my position in this world as the daughter of the highly esteemed Judge William Ferrell and his wife, Ester Lovenia, my mother. Mama was lovely: tall and elegant with striking blue eyes that twinkled when she smiled and long, silky hair the color of spun gold. A spark within her drew people, and she was well-loved within the community for her compassion toward others and the fabulous parties she threw on special occasions.

Our household staff was tremendously loyal and included the best cook in the county – as a result, everyone who graced our home enjoyed some of the most delectable desserts imaginable. Visitors were welcome, and they came frequently.

There was always a warm, inviting fire in our home during chilly days, and a cool breeze flowed through during the hot, sticky summer months. Papa rushed home every evening to bask in the loving glow of Mama's presence.

I had been Mama's constant companion on her outings, but our amazing adventures began to dwindle. The festive

A New Life

dinners with visitors ceased. I was too young to understand that illness had overtaken her, and my childhood eyes could not see her lovely frame begin to fail. Eventually, the illness swept her away from us, and the spark that made our home so welcoming departed.

Papa struggled with overwhelming grief when he came home. He hid away in the only room of our home that did not hold Mama's memories, his study. Before long, he was off traveling when he was not sitting on the Judge's bench. As a little girl, I only knew that my Mama was gone, and now Papa as well. I looked forward to his occasional visits, but each time he left, our home plunged into a lonely place again. Perhaps it was his guilt over abandoning me that he instructed the staff not to correct me for any reason. I was a forsaken little girl who grew up to resemble her beautiful Mother on the outside but without the spark that had produced compassion in her heart. My life began to change once more on an early spring morning. That was when dear Papa returned home from England.

"Grace! Grace!" Papa bellowed from the bottom of our stairway, which curved gracefully upward and around the grand foyer of our home. "Grace! Come here at once!" His deep baritone voice drifted throughout the empty rooms until it found me at practice with my music master, Mr. Bernard Hedges. "I have someone very important here whom I want you to meet!"

"It's Papa!" I exclaimed to Mr. Hedges. The music

master stood rather stoically at the end of our grand piano. "May I take your leave?" I mainly asked out of politeness rather than requesting permission. It was Papa beckoning me away.

"Why yes, of course, Miss Grace. We can resume the lesson tomorrow." The shrill staccato of his response betrayed annoyance.

The skirt of my green satin gown gave me a soft forewarning of what lay ahead: hush, but I gave it no mind and dashed down the upstairs hallway to greet Papa. At the head of the stairs, I stopped short. Papa had brought home a visitor. Standing beside him was a young woman with flowing, raven-colored hair and the deepest emerald-green eyes I had ever seen. I pondered over the unexpected visitor. Who was she? Perhaps the daughter of a friend? Indeed, not a new servant – not with the expensive velvet dress and fine pearls that she adorned so well.

Not wishing to be rude, I smiled the most welcoming smile I could muster, then stepped slowly and gracefully down the spiral staircase to where they stood. Papa's face beamed in adoration.

"Grace, Grace," Papa cooed to me, his beloved only child. He clasped one of my hands in his. At the same time, he gently took one of the young woman's hands and held them both to his heart.

"Grace, my child, I would love to introduce my new wife and your new mother, Angela." This he announced as he gazed at the young woman with adoring eyes. Angela

A New Life

looked back at him with a shy, coquettish smile.

The unexpected announcement left me unprepared for a measured, polite response. "Your what?" I snatched my hand back and tightly clasped both behind my back to keep them from trembling. My emotions churned. I could only stand in the foyer, gawking at the two of them. Surely, either I had misunderstood Papa, or he had been joking!

Papa's voice sounded *very* displeased with my reaction. "My wife, I said. Angela is my new wife *and the mistress of our home. I am sure that you will give her both the respect and honor that she deserves.*" The latter statement he spoke with great emphasis, and a stern look.

I was aghast with the news. No letter or telegram had been sent to forewarn me of such a tremendous announcement. What type of reaction had he expected? Why, she was but a child compared to him! She could have been his daughter instead of a wife! Angela, the young woman who stood proudly beside him, attempted a sympathetic smile which I greatly detested.

"We shall be having guests tomorrow evening in celebration of our arrival home and to introduce Angela to everyone." Papa's statement was aimed at both me and Charles, our butler, as he entered the room. Charles was struggling with one of Angela's many steamer trunks. Fresh beads of perspiration dotted his pale forehead, plastering thinning strands of black hair to the top of his head.

"Yes, sir," Charles responded with a proper nod and a tug at the heavy trunk.

"I will expect to see you there to express your support and blessing." Papa had turned his attention back to me and spoke each word with great emphasis. I'd seen the expression on his face before – it was one that he used when lecturing a mischief-maker in his courtroom.

"Why yes, of course, Papa," I replied in a sweet, reconciling voice (which I did not really mean at the time). And with a respectable curtsy to Angela, I said, "Welcome, Angela. I hope that you will be happy here in your new home." It pleased Papa, of course, but it was the day that would change my life forever.

***

Just as he'd instructed, the grandest reception that our county had seen in years graced our home. String musicians were stationed in a corner nearest the front door to greet our guests, and Mr. Hedges, my music master, delighted them in the banquet room with his prowess for ivory keys. Our twin chandeliers which hung from the banquet room's ceiling, reflected translucent rainbows across the mural-painted walls. Imported Irish linen tablecloths were draped over long dining tables, and elaborately cut crystal vases had been filled with arrangements of dark pink roses – Angela's favorite flowers. A new set of fine English china graced each seat at the tables. They were accented by new ornate, sterling utensils and crystal water goblets. Each, no doubt, was a gift from Papa for his new bride.

Everyone was dressed in their finery – men in elegant black-tie and women in shimmering satin and soft velvet gowns embellished with fine lace and pearls. I had chosen to wear black satin – a gown that my own beloved Jerrold had said he adored, and my blonde hair twisted up onto the top of my head. One of Mother's favorite tiaras and several silver hair pins held each hair in its proper place.

It was a relief to see Jerrold when he finally arrived. I had not had the opportunity to speak to him since the shocking news of Papa's new bride, and I'd looked forward to the comfort he would undoubtedly give. He was dashing, arrayed in a silk, high-waisted black coat and tie, and as he strode confidently across the room toward me, all eyes turned to watch in admiration. My earlier woes were swept away.

"Oh, Jerrold!" I swooned and clung to his muscular shoulders, "Whatever shall become of us? When shall *we* be able to marry?"

"Soon, dear Grace, soon," he assured me, and he gently fingered a curled tendril of my hair. "Let's let them enjoy being newlyweds for a bit. In just a short, respectable time, we will also be wed and happy for the rest of our lives." This he said with an affectionate wink and a wide, disarming smile which took my breath away. Jerrold's confidence dissuaded my fears. After all, wasn't he the most brilliant solicitor of law in our great city? Papa frequently said so. Many thought that he would eventually take his place on the bench; but despite Jerrold's brilliant insight into such matters, it was not to be this time.

***

The morning had been fresh and crisp on that fateful day in April just a short week later. Papa had begun to resume his duties on the bench, and Angela entertained herself by increasing the wealth of the local shop merchants. Despite a new mistress in our home, things continued to run as usual. The relief felt by the entire household staff was palpable, and a special meal was planned for that evening. Our party mood was interrupted by a sudden clamor at the front door. Papa stood there, pale and gasping for air. He held his chest with one hand and weakly hung onto the doorway with the other. As quickly as Jerrold had winked his assurance, Papa was gone from us. It was a splendid funeral, I was told, but in my misery and grief, I did not remember a thing. Even as horrible as Papa's death was, the worst was yet to come.

***

Mr. Johnson sat rigidly in Papa's leather chair at his splendid mahogany desk in the study. He had been Papa's own attorney and best friend for years. His thick, graying hair was combed securely into place, and his small reading spectacles reflected the light from the oil lamp that hung above Papa's desk. He had called Angela, me, and Jerrold; Charles, and the two maids: Ella, who took care of the upstairs, and me, and Bessie, who cared for the downstairs, and cooking; and James, who cared for the stable, horses, and grounds.

Angela and I were seated in the fine leather chairs that faced Papa's desk. I sat quietly, numbed by my immense grief, and Angela sat sniffing into a fine, embroidered lace handkerchief that Papa had given her. Her expensive French perfume made me feel slightly nauseated.

Dear sweet Jerrold stood behind me. He rested his hands on my shoulders in a comforting gesture. The servants stood at attention in a semi-circle behind him, each of them with a common, grayish-white handkerchief dotting their reddened eyes, respectably. We were all there, waiting for Mr. Johnson to read Papa's last wishes.

"Angela," he began, in a deep, somber voice, "your husband, the late Judge Ferrell, has provided very well for your needs. After you arrived home last week, he came to me and wanted your new home, a handsome allowance, and servants provided for you, should something unforeseen happen to him." He then cleared his throat several times before he was able to continue. "Grace, because of your forthcoming nuptials to Jerrold, your father left a handsome dowry and his love and best wishes for you both."

Mr. Andrews' voice drummed on, but I did not hear any more. I was paralyzed in a numb stupor. A dowry? The only thing that dear Papa left me was a dowry. I could only sit staring straight ahead as the muffled sound of soft voices murmured gently around me.

***

Although I took to my bed, sleep was replaced with bouts of mournful crying that left me exhausted. Ella pulled the drapes around my bed to provide some privacy. I heard the clip of James' boots across the wooden floor, then a rustling sound as he stacked logs in the fireplace. Soon, the soothing crackle of a fire and warmth replaced the room's early spring chill. Ella and James whispered to each other – then Bessie joined them when she brought a tray of dinner and sat it on a table by the bed. It wasn't long before Charles entered the room and sent everyone out, then closed the door quietly behind him. I felt abandoned and alone and wept bitterly once more.

***

Just as it always does, life around me continued. The sun had risen and set three times outside my bedroom window. Ella stood at my bedside with another untouched tray of food in her hands. "Really, Miss Grace. You *must* eat something. Your father would want it," she insisted. After a short pause, I heard the pad of her soft footsteps and the click of the door as it closed behind her. As if on cue, my stomach rumbled.

For a moment, I allowed my thoughts to overtake me, and I groaned in agony, but there were no tears left to flow. My body ached and felt weak. For a few minutes, I laid still and listened. The house had become completely still, and for the first time in days, my thoughts were on food. I sat up and opened the bed's curtain, flipped the covers back, and eased my legs over the side. My head began to swim, then spin, but after a bit, the room finally settled.

Ella had left my blue dressing gown draped on the edge of the carved mahogany vanity just beyond the foot of the bed. I carefully slid off the bed, slipped on the dressing

A New Life

gown, and tied the sash. The reflection that stared back from the vanity mirror made me gasp: there were dark circles under my reddened eyes. My cheeks looked sunken and sallow. My hair was wild and unkempt. *No matter. Everyone should have gone to bed by now.* I quietly opened my bedroom door and tiptoed silently toward the rear staircase which led to the kitchen.

". . . and dear Lord, we ask that you please be with Grace as she mourns the loss of her earthly father. . ."

The faint sound of Charles' voice stopped me on the stairs. He'd spoken my name. The darkness and turn of the stairwell kept me hidden. It was not polite to listen, but I felt compelled to stay. "And Lord, we ask Your will for her life, whether it is with her fiancée Jerrold, or You choose to send her on another path. Most of all, we ask that if she does not know you as her Lord and Savior, You will reveal Yourself to her. Lord, we ask you to also comfort Angela in the loss of her husband," he continued.

Upon occasion, I could distinguish the voices of either Ella, Bessie, or James as they added requests or thanks or an 'amen' to the conversation. A final 'amen' from Charles closed the prayer.

"Bessie, let me help you with those," Ella offered. I could hear the clink of china as they gathered dishes.

"No, it's just a bit of dishes, but thank you," Bessie replied. "I can have these done in just a jiffy. You go head on to bed," she said. There was a small chorus of 'The pie was wonderful, Bessie', 'Thank you for the pie,' and 'Good nights,' along with the soft shuffle of exiting feet. Except for the sound of Bessie at work, the room fell silent.

I sat in the dark stairwell and listened until I was sure that Bessie was alone before entering the kitchen. She was at the sink, busy with her task, and totally unaware of my presence. "Is there any more pie left?" I croaked. My throat was dry. It gave her quite a start.

"Woo! Sweet Jesus!" she exclaimed. She held her hand over her heart – then smiled. "I sure do. A *big* piece with your name on it." She pulled a chair out for me at the table, filled the tea kettle with water, and set it on the stove. Just as she had promised, she scooped up a big piece of apple pie and set it on a plate in front of me. I began to devour it, although I felt guilty for the pleasure. Papa was in the ground. There would be no more apple pie for him.

"I listened to you praying," I eventually confessed. "I didn't mean to eavesdrop, but I heard my name."

"Yes, we are praying for you, Grace." She paused in thought. "This is a terrible time for you, but God understands your heartache. He loves you – we all do."

The tea kettle began to whistle, spitting a stream of hot steam from its spout. Bessie carefully grasped the handle and poured us both a cup of hot water, then pulled out a chair and sat directly across from me. She picked up the tea strainer and began to rhythmically dip it into my cup, then hers. When she finished, I added a spoonful of sugar and stirred it slowly. I thought about what she'd said: that God loved me.

"Then why did He let Papa die?" I asked. "If He loves me, why would he leave me all alone like this? I cannot bear it." My voice broke briefly with the weight of the words.

Bessie reached out and placed her warm hand on top of mine. "It does seem unfair, doesn't it? Terribly unfair." She reached for an old, worn Bible which sat on the edge of the table, opened and flipped through the pages before she turned it toward me. There was a long list of names: this person begat that person. They lived and they died. "Look at all these names, honey. Every single one of them had people that loved them and mourned at their passing. It's very sad. People live and they die. Sometimes they are very young. Sometimes, they've suffered with illness. Sometimes they leave little ones behind. But the heavenly Father knows them all," she explained. She looked sad. Perhaps she was thinking about Papa, too.

Since he had passed, I'd had a lingering question that continued to plague me. "Do you think Papa went to heaven?" I asked. "He was a good man. Wasn't he?"

Bessie smiled, but it was gentle and sad. "I believe that anyone who has ever laid a loved one to rest has wondered the same thing. Grace, both your Papa *and* Mama were good people," she stressed, "and they loved you more than life itself – you can be sure of that." She paused as if to search for the right words. "The Bible tells us that there is a certain time for everything, including death. We don't know when that time is for *us,* but God does. From the moment we are born, our days are numbered. Death doesn't come as a surprise to Him. He knows and counts every hair on our head," she explained.

I nodded and took a sip of my tea. Bessie stood up and poured more hot water into our cups. "Because God loves us so much, He made a way for us to spend forever with Him. God is perfect, but man is sinful. Everyone has done something they shouldn't have in their lives. That's just the way we're born. Man has a sinful nature. We sin and think that we got away with it, but that's not true. God knows everything." She picked up the tea strainer and dipped it several times in our teacups. Bessie drifted off in her own thoughts, and we sat quietly sipping hot tea. Finally, the grandfather clock in the drawing room clanged eleven times, and I wanted to hear the rest of the story: how God made a way for us to spend forever with Him. Bessie was still sitting quietly, sipping her tea.

"So, what did God do?" I prompted. "How can we know that we'll go to Heaven?"

"Sin comes with a price, Grace, just like breaking the law. If you steal something, you get punished by going to jail. You sin, you get punished as well," she explained. "Since God can't abide sin, He made a way for us to be sinless, and He did that through his son Jesus. Jesus took the punishment for every wrong thing that mankind has ever done and will *ever* do. He did this when He allowed them to nail him to the cross, but because He was also God in the flesh, death couldn't keep Him. The Bible tells us that He rose again on the third day. Because Jesus took the punishment *for* us, those who repent and turn away from their sin, and accept His sacrifice on the cross for the forgiveness of their sins are 'born again' and have a home waiting for them in Heaven." She paused. "God makes us a new person. Have you ever repented of your sins, Grace, and placed your trust in Him?" she asked. "He is the only way to heaven."

"No," I admitted. "I went to church with Mama, but I don't remember anyone explaining it like this." I stared at the table for a bit, deep in thought. "Do you think Mama and Papa are in Heaven?" I asked.

"I hope so," she said, "but I *do* know that it is God's will for everyone to go to Heaven, so He gives everyone the opportunity to accept Him during their lifetime. He lets us decide on our own. Would you *like* to accept Jesus, Grace?" Bessie asked. She had always been kind to me throughout the years. Her question did not offend me in the least.

"I'd like to think about it if you don't mind." I wanted to spend some time alone sorting things out about Mama and Papa, and what Bessie had spoken of.

"Of course, Honey." She patted my hand affectionately. "Imagine this," she smiled, and her eyes twinkled with excitement as she spoke. "You prepared a very special gift for someone and invited them over to pick it up. You might wait for a while – but after a time, if they never came, you'd decide that they must not be interested and offer it to another. They would have missed out on a wonderful blessing that you had for them." She paused. "Remember that our days are numbered. Perhaps today is *your* day to accept God's gift of life with Him in Heaven. The Bible says, 'Today is the day of salvation'. I'm here anytime if you want to talk." She smiled, then stood from the table and began to collect our dishes.

I slipped from the kitchen to the hallway, then toward the front of the house where Papa's study was. On most nights, the house would be dark, but gentle beams of light cast from a full moon gave everything a soft glow. The scent of fine leather, tobacco, and peppermint greeted me at the door. Everything was just as he'd left it, and as I stepped in, I touched his things: his scarf, hat, and overcoat, the carved ivory handle to his umbrella, and the cool, smooth top of his mahogany desk. I pulled his scarf from the coat rack and wrapped it around my neck to feel Papa's embrace. The desk's leather chair creaked softly as I eased down onto the coolness of the seat.

Papa must have been busy the morning of his passing. There were papers and envelopes scattered about the desk. I squinted to read some of the papers in the soft glow of the moonlit room, then closed my eyes and inhaled the lingering scent of Papa's expensive shaving soap. This moment was mine alone to spend with his memory. There was no Angela – a stranger in my childhood home – to steal it from me.

I began to open the desk drawers, drawers that I had explored curiously as a child. First the top left, the bottom, which held my dowry, then the top right drawer. In it was a worn leather book like Bessie's. On the front, the words: Holy Bible were printed in gold. Tucked inside the book's yellowing pages was a folded piece of paper. I took it out and carefully unfolded it. Papa's familiar scrawl filled the page. It was a letter that he had been writing to me.

'Dear Grace,' it began. *'Please forgive me for having surprised you with Angela without the courtesy of a letter prior to our arrival. I have been so lonely since your mother left us, and your upcoming marriage to Jerrold would have left me quite alone. I have thought much about the afterlife since your mother's passing, and I had begun to look for comfort in this old Bible that had been my mother's. The thought of being alone was such agony, and I had begun to pray for the company of another companion. No one could take the place of your dear mother, but I thought, surely, a God that can create the universe could find me someone to fill my remaining days.'*

The letter ended, perhaps before it had been entirely penned – but this I knew: Papa had been thinking of me, and he had also been reaching out to the God of the Universe. Papa had been speaking to God. I folded Papa's letter, placed it back into the Bible, and set off to find Bessie.

The kitchen was quiet and dark: tea towels had been hung to dry on the towel rack by the sink, and chairs were upside down atop the wooden table. The iron stove creaked softly as it cooled.

I quietly made my way down to Bessie's room and tapped on the door. "Bessie?" I whispered. "Are you still up?"

The door opened a crack, and Bessie, dressed in her nightgown, peered out. "Grace?"

"Yes," I replied. "Can I speak to you for a moment? I'd like to show you something."

"Of course. Of course." She opened her door wider and beckoned me in. "Come on in, Grace, and sit with me."

The room was simply furnished: a single bed with white sheets and quilt, a small dresser with a mirror, and a wash basin. Bessie sat on the bed and patted the spot next to her. I sat down, and the bed springs creaked softly.

"Look what I found in Papa's room." I handed her the worn, leather Bible. "There's a letter in it," I explained. "Papa was writing me a letter." I pulled on the edge of the paper, and it slid easily out from the book's thin pages. "Look what he wrote."

The room's only source of light, a clear oil lamp, cast a soft glow, and Bessie leaned toward the light and read quietly. Her lips moved silently as she read. When she finished, she carefully folded the paper and placed a warm hand atop mine. "I'm so glad that he left you this beautiful letter, Grace. This was your Grandmother's Bible?" It seemed like a statement rather than a question. She began to gently turn the thin, yellowed pages, then smiled and handed the book back to me. "Look at this, Grace." A line had been drawn underneath a passage in the book. It was drawn with Papa's ink pen. I studied it for a moment, then read it aloud:

"John one-twelve: But as many as received him, to them gave he the power to become the sons of God, even to them who believe on His name." I sat quietly, pondering the meaning of the words, and that Papa had taken the time to underline them. Soft, warm tears began to roll down my face, and I traced the precious words with my finger. "Bessie, I want to become a child of God, too," I confessed. "I have tried to be a good person, but I know that I have still sinned against God, and I need Him to forgive me. I believe, just as you said, that God's son Jesus died on the cross for my sins and that he came back alive. Bessie, I want to go to Heaven if I should die."

"Well, let's tell Him, then," Bessie said softly. She eased off the bed and slid down to her knees onto the coolness of the room's polished wood floor. I followed her lead.

"Jesus," I said, "I believe that you are the Son of God – that you died on the cross for my sins and that you rose from the dead. Please forgive me. I want to be a child of God."

Bessie reached out and squeezed my hand. "It's that simple," she said. I marveled silently that the sting of Papa's death suddenly felt lighter.

As the cool spring days rolled slowly by, I began to chastise myself over my selfishness. Of course, Papa would leave Angela a home. I would have my own spectacular home with Jerrold once we were married, and I was sure that we would have a fine wedding once we had waited a respectable amount of time. Dear Jerrold came by almost every day to comfort us, and I busied myself, making quiet plans for our forthcoming nuptials. But I began to hear discomforting talk behind my back as I went about town shopping and having tea with my friends.

One morning, I was in the dressmaker's shop looking at fine material for a wedding dress when I overheard two busybodies speaking softly to Mrs. Cornell, the dressmaker.

"We'll see just which one Mr. Jerrold will marry," one lady cackled. "He is going over there every day, biding his time . . . and the flower of Miss Grace's youth will soon be gone. Then where shall she be? One day a rich Judge's daughter, the cream of society – the next, a poor spinster woman pinching her pennies to live off a small dowry. Whatever could she do to support herself? She would be absolutely useless to anyone."

Then, the other lady added her own unscrupulous thoughts to the conversation. "Perhaps, the late Judge Ferrell's widow would give her a job cleaning chamber pots – or should I say, the soon-to-be Mrs. Jerrold Wilson," she said slyly, and the ladies laughed quietly together over their private conversation.

I slipped out the door as quietly as I could so that they could not get any satisfaction from the redness of my eyes or cheeks and hurried home as quickly as possible. Because of the conversation I overheard, I decided to test Jerrold and see what his reaction would be if I were to propose a speedy wedding.

***

  We sat on the large, wooden swing in the moonlit garden behind the house, swinging gently and enjoying the fragrant early spring breeze from our beautifully manicured gardens. Jerrold affectionately held my hand in his and occasionally brought it to his lips. I began to chide myself for having even listened to the silly busy bodies in the dressmaker's shop. What could they possibly know about us? They were merely on the outside looking in and had never so much as graced our doorstep.

  "Jerrold," I began in a soft, sweet way, "I know that it hasn't been very long since Papa passed away, but don't you think that we have waited so long already that we should begin planning our wedding together? I think that everyone would understand, don't you? I can hardly wait to be called Mrs. Jerrold Wilson and have a home of my own to make beautiful. We could invite our friends over for special gatherings, just like Mama did with our home. Oh, Jerrold! This just doesn't feel like my home anymore since Papa gave it to Angela. Couldn't we begin planning, Jerrold, please?"

  I felt ashamed once I got to the begging part, because all Jerrold could do was to stammer and stutter. I could see his cheeks grow red in the moonlight, and he even dropped my hand and began clasping and wringing his own together.

  "Grace," he stammered, "I don't believe that this is the proper time to discuss this . . . it just would not be seemly. I really must be going, sweetheart. I have to begin work early tomorrow." He stood quickly from the swing. "I will call for you and Angela early tomorrow evening to attend the charity gala at Twin Gates. Since it was your father's favorite event, do be a dear and be ready, won't you?" He gave my cheek a short peck and strode quickly away, leaving me alone in the garden to weep.

I decided to give Jerrold one last chance. Surely, he would not attend the gala without me, his betrothed, if I were too ill to attend, myself? Etiquette would insist that the plans to attend be canceled, and Jerrold would have to go back home, and Angela back to her room to change out of her beautiful gown.

I watched Jerrold alight from the elegant, black, open carriage that he brought to escort us to the dance. He was handsome as always, with his thick, wavy hair combed neatly back and dressed in a dark jacket with tails. His shiny black boots made sharp clipping sounds as he walked briskly down our red brick walkway to the front door. I could hear the crisp rapping of his familiar knock and could imagine Charles opening the door for him and Jerrold stepping gallantly into the brightly lit foyer.

Ella gently knocked on my bedroom door to announce that Jerrold had arrived to escort us. "Miss Grace?" she whispered in her soft voice. "Aren't you going this evening with Mr. Jerrold? He has arrived to take you and Mrs. Ferrell to the gala at Twin Gates. He's waiting in the foyer now."

"I'm sorry, Ella." I opened my door just a crack. "Would you please send my regrets to Jerrold for the evening? I'm not feeling well."

"Yes, ma'am." Her reply was soft and respectful. With a worried look that sent frown lines across her pale face, she turned to walk quickly down the carpeted hall to the stairs.

I could hear Angela's bedroom door open and close and her soft footsteps as she gracefully glided down the stairs of our elaborate spiral staircase to the foyer. I could imagine, with a smile, her disappointment when she was told that they would not be able to attend the gala that evening.

As the front door opened and closed again, I ran back to my window to peek at Jerrold as he climbed back into his carriage to leave for home. But through a veil of soft tears, I watched Angela and Jerrold walk arm-in-arm down the brick walkway of my lost childhood home. I could hear the dainty tinkling of Angela's soft laughter as she placed her head gently on his strong shoulder and the sharp, rhythmic clopping of the horse's hooves as they slowly drove down the circle driveway and into the dark spring night. Dear Jerrold. I guess he preferred a rich Judge's widow to an orphan's dowry.

If I had been in my right senses, I would have likely cast away my next decision: I was going to leave home and set out on my own. Surely, I could find a position somewhere, I reasoned, until I could find a suitable match for myself! Perhaps I could begin a young ladies' finishing school or become a governess for a rich family. Maybe I could even find a rich widower who was struggling to raise his young children, and I, with my fine upbringing and education, would sweep him off his feet and save the day. Of course, everyone, including his children, would simply adore me!

I slowly opened my bedroom door, careful not to allow it to squeak, and made my way silently down the spiral staircase to Papa's study. It was dark, but I knew every piece of furniture in it, and was very confident that I could feel my way around without lighting a candle or lamp. The faint laughter of the servants drifted musically across the house and into Papa's study, as they sat taking their dinner in the kitchen, together. Silently – with bated breath, I opened the heavy mahogany desk drawer where Mr. Johnson had placed my dowry and let out a silent breath of relief as I felt the familiar leather satchel in my hand. Afterward, I opened the drawer and took out Papa's Bible and the letter that he'd written me.

Suddenly, silvery beams from the full moon broke free from their cloudy prison, brightly illuminating the dark room. I looked around Papa's study, making a memory that would have to last a lifetime. I ran my fingers along his desk, felt the familiar ornate carvings on its sides, and inhaled deeply to smell the pungent scent of his oil lamps. Various letters and papers remained strewn across the top of his desk – no doubt things he had been reading the morning on which he died.

My gaze fell on the bold headline of Papa's *Gazette*: 'The Westward Trail: A New Beginning.' Why yes, of course, I thought to myself. I had heard Papa speak of those who left the city and traveled westward in search of a new life. Perhaps, this was God's way of telling me where to go. I tucked the *Gazette* securely under my arm, picked up Papa's Bible, and firmly grabbed the precious leather satchel containing my dowry. With a deep breath of determination, I walked with confidence out of his study and up the stairway to my room to pack.

I would have to carry whatever I took. The realization hit me as I looked at my large wardrobe of expensive clothing. It pained me deeply to decide to take only a few of my things; things which would fit into a bag small enough for me to carry myself. Of course, I took Mama's jewelry, but other than that, I could only fit some under things, two extra dresses, and an extra pair of shoes. I packed the Bible with Papa's letter and my dowry, then penned a short farewell note to Jerrold.

> *Dear Jerrold,*
> *I am relieving you of the*
> *responsibility of our engagement.*
> *I hope that we shall both find true*
> *happiness in life.*
> *Deepest regards, Grace*

I folded it carefully and laid it on my dresser, then straightened my hair and donned a lightweight cape. With a deep sigh, I picked up my bag and gazed around my childhood room. There was no need to look at it with regrets, I told myself. Today would begin a new adventure for me . . . perhaps something that I would look back upon with great amazement. I quietly slipped down the stairway to Papa's office and carefully laid my note to Jerrold on the desk. With our engagement no longer an obstacle, the desk would likely belong to him before long. Tears began to mist my eyes as I slowly slipped off the engagement ring that Jerrold had given me and placed it on the note. With my head held high, and travel bag firmly clasped in my hand, I walked proudly out of Angela's home, closing the door of my old life behind me.

Two
The Journey Begins

For I know the plans I have for you, declares the Lord, plans to prosper you and not to harm you, plans to give you hope and a future.
Jeremiah 29:11

    The brisk spring night refreshed my senses as I silently made my final walk down the red brick walkway. I could remember the many times as a child, that Mama held my tiny hand when we made this same journey together. My short legs had to trot quickly to keep up with her graceful, elegant strides. The walkway had been so long back then. This evening, it seemed particularly short, and I found myself standing in the street like a commoner waiting for a taxi to pass by. A black hansom cab, drawn by a well-groomed chestnut, made its way down the dimly lit street and slowed to a halt in front of me.
    The driver appeared chestnut as well, with his own mane of wiry, red hair stuffed securely under a black derby hat. A black wool coat kept him warm from the evening chill, and his tall boots, shined to perfection, were a less-expensive imitation of Jerrold's. He smiled, and a pair of gentle brown eyes looked down from the perch of his cab.
    "Gud eve'nin, Ma'am." He spoke with a thick, crisp, Irish accent and quickly hopped down from his seat. "Where might I take ye on such a brisk eve'nin as this?"
    Struggling against uncertainty, I lifted my chin,

straightened my back, squared my shoulders, and responded, "I would like to go to Central Station, please."

"Yes, ma'am," he replied politely.

I had never traveled at night without an escort before and felt quite nervous about it. For a moment, I pictured Jerrold and Angela dancing together and winced. The pain that it inflicted gave me the courage to continue. I handed the driver my gray leather bag, stepped carefully up into the cab, and then slid across the cool, dark leather seat.

He placed my bag on the floor, closed the door, and then jiggled the handle to ensure it had latched. The cab rocked slightly as he climbed back onto his seat – then a shrill whistle to the mare sent the cab suddenly forward with a slight jolt.

Alone again, I took time to reflect on the evening's events: Jerrold and Angela, the *Gazette* on Papa's desk, my decision to set out on my own, the letter I'd penned to Jerrold. Dear Papa's *Gazette* was still tucked securely under my arm. I unfolded it imagining that I could feel the strong hands which held it on the morning he departed. The tall gas lamps along the road intermittently brightened and then darkened the inside of the cab as we passed quickly by them.

"Flow'ars! Flow'ars!"

I leaned forward to gaze out the cab's window and glimpsed a poorly clad flower woman standing alone on a street corner. Her small wooden cart, which was filled with bundles of brightly colored flowers, sat next to her. I

The Journey Begins

wondered if Jerrold had stopped and purchased flowers for Angela, as he had done for me so many times before.

I settled back into the dark leather upholstery of the cab once more, took a deep breath of crisp night air, and exhaled with a sigh. It was time to leave the heartache of the past behind me. I would only take the memory of Mama and Papa and my newfound faith in God.

As we cruised along, I found that the rhythmic crescendo of clopping hooves as other cabs passed by and the melodic song of harnesses jingling was soothing. Occasionally, Cabbie would call out to others with whom he was familiar with:

"Gud eve'nin to ya! How's yer wife and cheld'ran? Yer rig looks smart this eve'nin!"

His cheery voice and friendly banter lifted my spirits. Occasionally, a friendly jab at another cabbie brought a slight smile to my lips – something that I was sure had been forsaken forever.

The cab came to a rocking stop, and he appeared at the cab's door to assist me. "Here ye are ma'am. Roit here at Centraw Stashun, just as ye asked."

I stepped down from the cab and paid him a handsome sum for his services.

"Thank ye, ma'am! God bless ye on yer journey!" he said. He tipped his hat in appreciation.

I picked up my bag and walked apprehensively toward the main door of the station as the hoof beats of Cabbie's horse slowly faded into the noise of the city's bustling nightlife. A tall, muscular policeman with dark, wavy hair stood beside the entrance door to the station.

"Good evening, ma'am." He greeted me with a friendly nod, then opened the heavy glass, mahogany-framed door.

"Thank you, sir." I returned his nod and shuffled past him into the main entrance of the train station. The large, brightly lit room was bustling with humanity.

There were people of various ages, races, and backgrounds moving in and out of the enormous building. Some were quite obviously in a hurry to catch their train, trotting awkwardly through the main building lugging baggage. Others were casually strolling about, laughing and talking lightheartedly with their traveling companions in anticipation of their upcoming adventure. I stood back, quietly observing the circus around me.

A short line of anxious people waited to be served at the ticket booth by a small, slightly balding gentleman. At the front of the line, a very robust man was busy waging war on the railway business.

"Like I said, Sir, the train had to leave on time. I'm sorry that it couldn't wait for you. I would be more than happy to exchange your ticket for another time," the man in the ticket booth reasoned.

"I don't want another ticket! I needed to be on that train," the large man roared. His face turned a deep, cherry red, and his hands intermittently clenched open and closed.

"Yes sir. I understand," the ticket master responded in a futile attempt to calm him. "But the train has left the

The Journey Begins

station."

"But I needed to be on that train!" His statement elicited a low moan from the crowd behind him. They were rescued when a crisp-looking young officer in a blue uniform politely took the gentleman gently but firmly by the elbow.

"Sir, would you please step this way," he commanded politely.

The man, looking somewhat bewildered, gently padded along like a lamb. The action prompted a lighthearted round of applause from those anxiously awaiting their turn.

"Next!" the small, bespectacled gentleman who stood behind the ticket booth shouted. The line moved up slightly as the next person in line, a dashing young man in a dark, expensive suit, stepped forward.

I quietly slipped behind the last person in the ticket line to await my turn. Directly in front of me stood a very tastefully dressed young woman in a blue linen dress and matching shoulder cape. Her thick, dark hair was twisted up into a halo that framed her creamy, delicate face; a lovely little girl with brown ringlets that cascaded down her back, stood quietly beside her. In front of them was a young couple dressed in elegant traveling attire. The woman's massive brown hair was neatly swept up into a fashionable twist. It was topped by a small purple hat adorned with a few smart-looking peacock feathers. It matched a purple dress that peeked from under the long black cape she wore. The gentleman wore a dark-colored expensive overcoat and pants made from fine, imported tweed. He had a hat that covered his thick, well-groomed brown hair. They were quite obviously in love. Standing arm in arm, they took turns whispering softly with affectionate smiles. Could it be that they were traveling to some distant place following a beautiful wedding? The thought saddened me.

"Next!" shouted the ticket master. The young couple moved up to the bars and began to speak with him in low, muffled tones.

"Are we next?" The little girl in front of me asked the young woman. As she spoke, her dark ringlets swung softly like long cylinder bells.

"Yes, we certainly are," the woman explained. She smiled at the child, and her face glowed with affection. The little girl yawned and rubbed droopy eyelids with her hands. Her angelic blue eyes, rimmed with thick, dark eyelashes, were slightly reddened from the late hour. With a deep sigh, she clung to the young woman's blue skirt.

"Next!" The young woman picked up two tapestry bags and moved up to the window.

I would be next. Where would I tell him that I wished to go? In my haste, I had no plan. Anger replaced my pain. Jerrold was the object of it.

"Next!" I stepped obediently forward to the ticket booth.

"Good evening, ma'am," the man behind the ticket window greeted me politely. "What can I do for you?"

"I would like to buy a train ticket," I stated factually. I took a moment to straighten the skirt to my dark green dress and smooth back my slightly frizzy hair. The night air was not doing it much good.

"Yes, ma'am! That's what I'm here for," he said. His voice sounded weary. "Where would you like to go?"

"I would like to go as far west as you can possibly get me." As I spoke, I cautiously reached into my bag for dowry money to pay for my ticket purchase.

"Well, ma'am – " the gentleman pondered as he looked at his map and train schedule. "I can get you as far as St. Louis, Missouri," he offered. You'd have a slight layover in Erie. If you wanted to go further, you would have to switch trains and could go to either Jefferson City or Marshall."

Decisions. I had made so many of them in such a short while. "Might I be able to purchase those tickets at the St. Louis station?" I inquired. "I'm unsure which route I would like to take right now."

He looked at me with a curious expression, then nodded. "Yes, ma'am, you certainly can. The price of the ticket to St. Louis would be thirty dollars.

I slipped a large bill under the iron bars of the booth.

"Thank you, ma'am." He slid the precious ticket and her change back under the protective bars. "Your train won't leave for another hour, but you can board now if you wish."

I thanked him genuinely, and after carefully tucking the ticket into my travel bag, I walked toward the trains. How did Papa figure out where to go? There were people and trains everywhere I observed. I finally spotted a young police officer and decided to ask for help.

"Excuse me, sir. Can you tell me where to catch my

train? I'm going to St. Louis." I quickly retrieved the ticket from my bag.

He was an attractive young man about my age, with sandy blonde hair and blue eyes. He was slightly stocky, in a muscular sort of way. At first, he looked only at my ticket as if this were a mundane chore, but when he glanced up, the expression on his face changed.

"Why yes, ma'am." He spoke slightly louder than was necessary. "I would be glad to help you find your train!"

I suspect that I received more attention from him that day than the average passenger did.

"Excuse me!" He parted passengers much like God had parted the Red Sea. I was embarrassed by the attention. Everyone looked at me with great curiosity, as if I might be someone very important to receive a personal police escort. "Here you are, ma'am." He gallantly placed me in the protective, capable hands of a stout conductor. "Would you see that Miss . . ." he trailed off, awaiting me to state my name.

"Miss Grace Ferrell," I replied.

"That Miss Ferrell gets safely to her destination of St. Louis?" He asked with great authority.

"Yes, sir, I certainly will." The conductor responded with a welcoming smile.

"Miss Ferrell, I certainly wish for you to have a safe journey. If you happen to get back to New York sometime in the future, would you please do me the honor of looking me up? My name is Officer Thomas Hartley."

The Journey Begins

"Why yes, I certainly will," I replied with downcast eyes. *But I will never be back*, I thought as I stood at the door to the train car.

He smiled and tipped his hat politely. We were interrupted by an older woman who wished his assistance, as well. I took the opportunity to escape and slipped quickly into the ladies' car to rest.

The train car consisted of a long, rectangular wooden box with pairs of brown leather seats facing each other on either side of a central aisle. Windows ran along both sides of the train and could be raised and lowered by the passengers. In the back of the car was a small closet where one could relieve oneself if necessary, a wooden water bucket with a common cup, and a small, wood-burning stove that was not in use.

The ladies' car was nearly empty, except for two elderly silver-haired women and the young woman with the small girl who had been in front of me at the ticket line. The elderly ladies were chatting quietly in their seats at the far end of the coach. The young woman smiled warmly when she saw me enter the train car. The small dark-haired child was fast asleep on the bench next to her – with her head lying peacefully across the young woman's lap. Soft, black eyelashes framed her small rose-kissed cheeks, and her tiny pink mouth was pursed into a dream-induced pout. A multi-colored quilt was securely tucked around her.

I motioned to the bench area next to them. "Do you mind if I sit here?"

"No, not at all," the young woman responded with a smile. "I would certainly enjoy the company."

I settled in next to them, tucked my bag securely under the seat, and lovingly spread Papa's wrinkled *Gazette* across my lap.

"My name is Violet," the young woman stated softly. "What is your name?"

"Grace," I answered with a smile. "Grace Ferrell."

"Nice to meet you," she said with a friendly nod. The little girl stirred, and Violet lovingly patted the child's shoulder.

"Is she your daughter?" I asked curiously.

"I'm her Governess," Violet said softly. "We're returning home to St. Louis after visiting her grandmother in New York for a few weeks. How far will you be going?" Violet's question was a near whisper.

"I'm not sure," I replied. The late hour made me feel suddenly tired, and I suppressed a yawn. "I have a ticket to St. Louis. I'm planning to go as far west as possible."

Violet's eyebrows lifted in curiosity, but even if she wished to know more, she chose not to ask any further questions. She busied herself, tucking the covers around the child again, and gazed out the open train window at the other travelers. Grateful for the silence, I took the opportunity to read the article about westward travel in Papa's *Gazette*.

The Journey Begins

The Westward Trail: A New Beginning
President Lincoln's Homestead Act spurred an increase in westward movement, promising 160 acres apiece to any man or woman, U.S. citizen or emigrant, who would occupy and improve the land for five years.
One of the major drawbacks to his settlement plan has been the extreme hardships that one must face, and many have returned, half-starved and penniless, before having even seen the promised land. It has been reported that massacres and Cholera have wiped out entire wagon trains. One cannot help but wonder if the President's plan to expand the states' territory as far west as the Pacific Ocean is utterly in vain . . .

Massacres and Cholera. That was certainly not something that I had anticipated. Who would mourn for me if I died? Who would know? This new revelation caused me to begin the all-consuming job of balancing the benefits of westward travel versus the drawbacks. What would I have to look forward to if I were to stay in St. Louis?

I looked at Violet. She continued to gaze sleepily out of the open train window. I could become a Governess like her and raise someone else's child, but I would have to do their bidding until they either wearied of me, or the child grew too old for one. Poor Violet. Perhaps, in some households, she might be treated as a member of the family . . . but in the home where I grew up, she would have been just another servant. I suddenly felt sorry for how I had treated

Ella, Bessie, Charles, and James over the years.

I could always open a finishing school for young ladies, I speculated. I could rent a fashionable building and have a fine sign painted over the doorway: Grace Ferrell's Finishing School for Young Ladies. I began to reminisce about my days at Miss Tilden's Ladies' Finishing School. Some of us were there to learn how to refine our manners so that we could impress notable people for our husband's benefit. Then, there were the other girls – unruly girls who had been brought by their parents because they could do nothing with them, themselves. I remembered poor Miss Tilden struggling to keep order within the group and teach lessons to those of us who wished to learn. I suspect that she would have sent those unruly girls packing, except for the ever-present necessity of money. For parents to send their daughters to her, it was important to keep a very high standard of living and dress. The higher the standard of living, the more expenses incurred, and the more tuition money was needed to pay for them. Hence, Miss Tilden struggled constantly to keep her patience and good manners with these incorrigible girls. Except for training of young women at the school, Miss Tilden seldom ever ventured out and was never courted. Poor lonely Miss Tilden! It had appeared a promising idea, but the more I reflected on it, it seemed to shout the word spinster – a fate which I hoped would not befall me!

My next thought was to marry well. How would one go about doing that? Could one place an ad in the paper

The Journey Begins

reading: Looking for one wealthy gentleman: not too terribly old, good-looking, who is searching for a well-educated, refined woman, for matrimony. Servants are a must! I frowned. Of course, I couldn't place an ad – and becoming a mail-order bride was even more so out of the question. I could possibly be paired with an ancient, gold-mining gent with a life-long sentence of cooking over a hot stove. That was not for me!

The only option that seemed acceptable was to continue to travel west and take the President up on his Homestead Act. It was an all-or-nothing venture. I would either succeed and settle my 160-acre plat, or I would die trying with no one to mourn me.

Where should I begin my journey westward? Once in St. Louis, I could purchase a ticket to either Marshall or Jefferson City, Missouri. I pondered the two choices: Marshall or Jefferson City. The name Marshall reflected law and order – it was thus that I decided on Marshall.

A deep rumble came from the train's engine, then white clouds of steam began to billow past the soot-covered train windows, signaling that our journey was about to begin.

"All aboard!" the Conductor's voice boomed beyond our train car.

I leaned back and firmly grasped the arm of the bench seat. I was a bit anxious, and reports of accidents did not help the matter much. I had overheard horror stories of trains plummeting downward from rotten bridges and exploding violently into a fiery mass of wood and steel.

There were other stories of trains in head-on collisions, the fault of the engineers not timing their routes correctly, or the track not switching as it should. I was slightly sorry that I had spent time eavesdropping on Papa's after-dinner conversations with gentlemen guests. The stories had seemed much more entertaining than embroidery. Besides, I had thought back then, who needed to do such things when one had servants to do them for you?

My gaze drifted to the small, dark-haired child who slept peacefully across the train aisle. There she was, safe and secure in her dreamland, with a loving Governess to care for her and both parents anxiously awaiting her return.

Violet turned from the window and smiled. Even she, a servant, had someplace to go home to. I smiled cordially, slowly closed my eyes, and rested my head on the back of the seat. Exhausted by my ordeal and lulled by the train's gentle rocking, I slept undisturbed until the next morning.

Three
Breakfast in Erie
Surely God is my help; the Lord is the one who sustains me.
Psalm 54:4

"Erie! Next stop Erie!" the conductor shouted as his large frame casually lumbered through the lady's car. He touched the back of the seats as he made his way slowly down the narrow aisle to steady himself against the train's jerking motion.

I opened my eyes slowly against the morning light and saw that a fine sheet of soot and ashes had settled over us during the night.

Violet smiled apologetically. "I'm sorry," she said. "As soon as the ashes began to blow in, I closed the window as quickly as possible. I'm afraid that I wasn't quite quick enough!"

The little girl began to stir from the commotion and was sitting straight up by the time the conductor reached our seats.

"Sir," Violet asked politely, "how long will we be here before we leave for St. Louis?"

"Exactly one hour!" He shouted the information above the rumble of the train cars and the locomotive's roaring engine.

"Thank you," Violet replied, and she began to shake the soot from the child's rumpled clothing.

The conductor continued toward the vestibule, which joined us to the other train cars.

"I think that we shall get out and stretch our legs, Grace. Would you care to join us?" she asked.

"Yes, I certainly would." I was grateful for someone to stroll with during our stop.

With a loud screech, the train suddenly began to vibrate and slow, sending great billows of white steam rolling past our ash-covered window. The little girl climbed quickly across Violet's lap and gazed out in wide-eyed amazement.

Violet laughed and gave the child a gentle hug as she helped to steady her from the train's unruly lurching.

"Nicole, I would like you to meet a new friend of ours. This is Miss Grace Ferrell."

The little girl turned momentarily to give me a brief smile, then immediately went back to her intense sight-seeing. Her long ringlets had survived the night, and short, soft, wispy curls caressed her angelic face. Thick, black eyelashes framed inquisitive blue eyes, and her mouth was opened wide in amazement.

The Erie station slowly lumbered into view, and mountains of thick, white steam engulfed the platform and train causing the awaiting passengers to temporarily disappear. "Watch your step, Sir! I hope that you had a comfortable trip!" We could hear the conductor from beyond our own train car.

"Shall we go?" I brushed as much of the ashes from my clothing as possible. Violet quickly gathered their things which had been displaced around them throughout the night. I had only my gray leather bag, my cape, and Papa's *Gazette* to carry. For the first time, I was glad to be traveling light and that I had left the wardrobe of heavy gowns behind.

What would be going on at home this morning, I wondered. By now, Ella had gone to my room to wake me for breakfast and found it empty – my bed still undisturbed during the night. There would have been a quick search of the house, and my note to Jerrold found on Papa's desk in the study. Perhaps Angela would feign a brief tirade of tears and sorrow. Someone might be sent to fetch Jerrold, and eventually, the household would settle back down to their daily routine. After all, what else was there to be done? I was an adult and could come and go as I pleased. I was sure, sadly, that Angela and Jerrold would be relieved of my departure – especially dear Jerrold. It cleared the way for his relationship with Angela, and he could now pretend that his visits were to comfort her in her abrupt, unexpected loss of a daughter. It would not fool those whose tongues wagged, nor the servants, though. He was foolish indeed if he thought so.

"Grace!" Violet laughed. She waved an arm to get my attention. "We are ready to go." She had a tapestry bag in each hand, and Nicole's little hands were firmly attached to her blue linen skirt.

"Yes, of course!" I was embarrassed that Violet had been forced to awaken me from daydreaming as if I were a schoolgirl.

She appeared so well in control of everything: intelligent, attractive, and with fine manners. Why on earth was she in a servant-type position and not married? I shook my head at the injustice and gathered my things.

We slowly walked down the aisle toward the vestibule, where the conductor was helping the elderly ladies step down. "Watch yer step, ladies!" he instructed crisply. They nodded gratefully and, once safely down onto the platform, walked quickly into the small clapboard station.

"Good morning, little miss!" he chirped to Nicole. "Let me hold your hand and help you down from the car so that you don't fall and hurt yourself!"

She clung tighter to Violet's skirt, almost disappearing into the generous folds of blue material. Violet wobbled dangerously from the tugging as she struggled to keep her balance, all the while holding onto the two heavy bags.

The conductor swiftly reached out and grabbed Violet's elbow to steady her. "Ladies, allow me to take your luggage."

I gratefully handed him my gray leather bag and stepped aside, so that Violet could give him their baggage, also. It was a blessing to be relieved of the cumbersome burden.

After putting our baggage onto the wooden platform, the conductor turned his attention back to us. "This way, ma'am!" He reached up and clasped my hand, then assisted me down the train's narrow, steep steps.

Violet slowly moved down as well, using one hand to

Breakfast in Erie

steady herself and the other to steady Nicole. With considerable effort, they were both safely planted on the platform.

"Shall we go inside and freshen ourselves?" Violet leaned down and picked up the heavy baggage from the platform.

"Yes, of course." I nodded in agreement.

The Erie station consisted of a simple, white clapboard, two-story building with ample windows for lighting and a sturdy metal roof. The upper floor of the building served as the Station Manager's home, where a row of four tow-headed, cleanly scrubbed faces peeked curiously through the open windows. The downstairs served as the train station and was divided into two large rooms: one which served as the ticket and telegraph room, the second as a lobby with two long wooden benches for passengers to await the arrival of their train. Two smaller rooms, the gentlemen's and ladies' water closets, were located at the far end. The most significant destination for us was the water closet room.

The room was surprisingly clean and fresh, a quality which could be credited to the Station Manager's wife, no doubt. The simple room provided a washstand, which held a large white bowl and a bucket of clean water for washing, and a small closet, where one could relieve oneself in private. Fortunate to be the only ones to use the room, we took full advantage of the facilities, relieving ourselves and washing the soot and dust from our faces and arms as best we could. We were even able to comb our hair and make ourselves more suitable in front of a large mirror. Violet opened one of their bags and changed Nicole into a fresh outfit: a blue and white striped dress with a white oval collar and soft, cotton petticoat. Much more presentable to the world, we picked up our bags and stepped out into the bright sunshine of the station lobby.

A young ginger-headed boy with bare feet ran quickly from the sidewalk into the station to greet us. "Good mor'nin ma'ams. Are you ladies gow'in to be staying here in Erie? Thay'rs a really nice hotel across the street whare you can get a nice room and have a hot meal."

"Thank you, but we will not be staying," Violet responded kindly. She took a penny from her skirt pocket and handed it to the boy. He smiled in appreciation and quickly scampered out the station door. We could hear his voice drifting into the station's doorway a few moments later:

"Good mor'nin sir. Are you gow'in to be staying here in Erie? Thay'rs a really nice hotel across the street whare you can get a nice room and have a hot meal."

Violet and I shared a giggle. The Station Manager, a tall, dark-haired gentleman with small spectacles, peeked out of his office door.

"That's Elvin Johnson. A real nice, polite boy. Got the reddest hair that I've ever seen. The people at the hotel pay him to advertise to train travelers when the train stops here.

We could hear his small voice faintly in the distance:

"Good mor'nin Sir. . ."

An elderly woman with rows of pale, wrinkled skin and thin white hair stepped carefully into the station. She wore a simple blue bonnet tied neatly under her chin and a faded, well-worn, green cotton dress. Nearly useless, her blue eyes were glazed and milky, and the few remaining teeth she had were stained brown from tobacco.

Ladies," she began slowly, with a slight slur, "I couldn't help overhearing the Station Manager speaking to you. I have a cart with some fine food out here if you'va mind to be eating sometime soon."

"I'm hungry," Nicole complained, tugging on Violet's blue skirt.

She looked up at her Governess with imploring eyes.

"Very well," Violet sighed. "We do have some fruit in our bags, but let's see what she might have to offer. Grace, would you like to join us?" She stood from the hard, wooden bench she had been resting on.

My stomach growled in complaint as well. In my haste to leave home, I hadn't given any thought to food. I longed for Bessie's shortbread and pancakes, which had been served, no doubt, at home this morning. I had serious doubts that I'd find anything in the cart very appetizing, but there wouldn't be another chance to purchase anything else until we arrived in St. Louis.

"Yes, thank you. I believe that I would," I replied and rose slowly from the bench on which I'd sat.

The elderly woman gave us a wide, jack-o-lantern smile and disappeared out of the station doorway. We casually strolled across the station's cleanly swept wooden floor and out into the bright sunlight of Erie.

Erie was a busy port town with wagons traveling everywhere quickly, heavy-laden with goods marked for ship and ferry travel. Throngs of people, some carrying packages and others empty-handed, moved up and down the wooden sidewalk, going about their daily business.

The hotel young Elvin had spoken of was directly across the street from where we stood. It was a large, two-story building with fancy white columns flanking an elaborate, stained-glass doorway. On the hotel's second floor was a sunny, picturesque veranda with fancy wrought-iron tables and vases with clusters of brightly colored wildflowers. A large picture window along the sidewalk below allowed one to watch the restaurant's customers consume a hearty breakfast. My stomach growled for a second time as I gazed longingly and wished that I could join them. It was a shame that we wouldn't have time to eat there.

The elderly woman had a small, bright blue wooden cart sitting directly outside the station doorway. In the dirt next to the walkway, she had built a small fire and had a steaming pot of aromatic coffee warming over it. The conductor, who had already taken full advantage of her goods, was sitting on the platform in the front of the station, finishing a meal of sweetbread and drinking a large tin cup of dark coffee.

Violet, who always appeared to be well-focused, was standing by the woman's cart, purchasing breakfast for her

Breakfast in Erie

and Nicole. Nicole was waving her little hands about and hopping up and down with excitement. Violet turned and handed Nicole a sweetbread in the form of a bunny.

"There you go, honey," she said. "One breakfast bunny. Be careful not to drop it!"

Nicole took a hungry bite of her bunny. She smiled widely, closed her eyes, and happily rocked back and forth as she savored the sweetbread slowly. Each bite elicited the same joyful, rocking ritual. Within a few short minutes, the bunny had been consumed entirely. Not to miss any of its sweetness, she commenced inserting each individual finger into her small mouth to suck the sugar off it and withdrew it with a small popping sound until all fingers had been thoroughly cleaned.

Violet had purchased sweetbread for her own breakfast and was busy tucking a few extras, which had been carefully wrapped in brown paper, into one of the tapestry bags for later. Taking my cue from everyone else, I stepped up to the blue cart to order breakfast.

"I would like two sweetbreads, please. Would you mind wrapping one of them for later?" I asked.

"Yes, ma'am." She carefully reached inside her cart and handed me one sweetbread – then wrapped another for me in brown paper as I'd asked.

"That'll be five cents." She stretched out a trembling, bony hand to receive her pay, revealing five twisted, gnarled fingers with thick, yellow nails.

I discreetly reached into my bag and paid the woman,

tipping her an extra penny for her trouble.

"Thank you, ma'am." She responded with a grateful nod, then turned away to tend to her goods.

The train's locomotive began to hiss loudly as it began to steam up for the trip to St. Louis. I looked about me, and noticed that the conductor had disappeared, and Violet and Nicole were nowhere to be seen, as well. Gripping the sweetbread, Papa's *Gazette*, and my gray leather bag tightly, I quickly rushed into the station's waiting room.

I breathed an audible sigh of relief when I spied Violet leading a freshly washed Nicole from the lady's water closet. "Oh, thank goodness!" I exclaimed. "I could imagine that I was going to be left behind!"

Violet smiled as she straightened Nicole's collar. "I promise not to let the train leave without you," she laughed softly. "You have been so preoccupied, Grace, that I think you need a Governess, too!"

Nicole began to giggle. "I'll share Violet wiff you."

"Why, thank you, Nicole. I appreciate your generous offer." I smiled at the small, dark-haired angel staring up at me from the folds of Violet's skirt.

Suddenly, the train whistle sounded, the engine began to roar, and plumbs of white steam billowed up into the air.

"All aboard!" the conductor shouted in a clear, booming voice. He stood on the station platform by the ladies' car, anxiously awaiting our arrival.

"I think if we don't hurry, we shall all get left behind!" Violet exclaimed. She grabbed their bags, and we quickly rushed out of the station to board the train.

"I wondered if you two ladies were going to join us for the rest of the trip," the conductor teased. His friendly smile widened the rows of pale wrinkles on his rough, whiskery face.

We quickly stepped off the station's wooden platform, where the conductor assisted us to board.

The train's engine soon began to rumble louder. Another *toot* from the whistle signaled the conductor. He waved at the engine and climbed on board. The Erie station slowly began to inch backward until it finally disappeared, and lovely, picturesque views whisked quickly past us.

Satisfied that we were well-settled, the conductor strolled up the train aisle until he slipped cautiously through the next car door, leaving us happily to fend for ourselves. Alone, refreshed, and with full tummies, we did the unthinkable – we took our shoes and stockings off, boldly revealing a wiggling row of thirty pink toes.

Four

A Sister and a Hat

For whosoever shall do the will of my Father which is in heaven, the same is my brother, and sister, and mother. Matthew 12:50

The trip from Erie to St. Louis was long and tiring, but we were seldom bored. We played little games with Nicole and allowed her to lead us in some children's songs. Violet had a beautiful, soft voice. She was not shy about singing, but the sweet melody which passed from her rose-colored lips, struggled to be heard above the loud din of the locomotive's engine. Taking her lead from Violet, little Nicole sang too, and swung her arms about while conducting her two-person choir. On the other hand, I had seldom sung in front of others. My singing had been mainly to myself while alone. I wasn't even sure that it was suitable for others to listen to, and was very content to sing softly, grateful to be overshadowed by the roar of modern-day train travel. When we tired of playing and singing, we unwrapped the sweetbread which had been purchased in Erie, and Violet unpacked some apples and bananas that she had brought. We carelessly picnicked on our laps, sucking on our fingers, just as Nicole had earlier. Miss Tilden, at the finishing school, would have fainted to see me abandon all manner of civility. The rest of the trip we either napped or wiled the time away, sharing bits of information about

A Sister and a Hat

ourselves. Violet freely spoke about her life and explained how it was that she came to be a Governess.

While she was still very young, Violet's mother became the head housekeeper of a great estate, named Ivy Hill. The mistress there was a very kind, and generous Christian woman, and quickly became fond of her. When she found that she had a little girl her own daughter's age, she generously insisted that Violet come every day with her mother to be a companion for her own daughter, Rebecca. Violet and Rebecca became very close friends, a relationship which continued onward to that very day. Violet was with Rebecca every minute possible, and because they were nearly inseparable, Violet received the benefit of a fine education from Rebecca's tutors, as well. When Rebecca became betrothed and married a fine young banker, she insisted that Violet, who was her only sister, come and stay with them. Later, when Rebecca gave birth to a precious dark-haired baby girl, she could suffer only Violet herself, to care for her child they had named Nicole.

It was a very sweet story, and it brought bittersweet tears to my eyes as I listened intently. How precious it would have been to have had a sister of my own to share my childhood with! I was so young when Mama became very ill and passed away. How I wished that they would have found me a companion like Violet. Our large home had been so empty, and we had so much to offer.

I shared the things which had transpired in my life the last few weeks: about dear Papa bringing home Angela, his untimely death, and Jerrold's infatuation with Papa's estate. She was kind and sympathetic, nodding quietly when appropriate and frowning deeply with concern when it was needed. It was indeed pleasant to have someone to talk to. The young women back home, whom I referred to as friends, were merely acquaintances. They were friendly toward me because of Papa's notable position and the grand parties that he hosted when home. But there was something very different about Violet. We had a few moments of quiet while Nicole slept. I decided to broach the subject.

"Violet," I began, not quite sure how or what to ask, "you are so different. I mean, there is something so special about you. You are not at all like my friends back home!" I was sure that I sounded rather foolish. Violet just smiled sweetly and gently clasped my hand in friendship.

"When I was very young, Rebecca's mother would read Bible stories to us, and I often attended church services with them. She loved to tell everyone how the Lord, Jesus Christ, made a difference in her life and how He wanted to be the Lord of our lives, too. When I was old enough to understand, I decided to ask Jesus to be my Savior and forgive me of my sins. Rebecca did too! We promised to be forever friends, just like Jonathan and David were, in the Bible. We made a pinkie promise by hooking our fingers together and reading the promise Jonathan and David made to each other in the Bible!" She held her hands up, with her two smallest fingers hooked together, laughing gently as she remembered.

"Have you ever asked Jesus to forgive you of your sins and be your Savior?" she asked with a smile.

"Yes!" I shared how I had overheard the staff praying for me while I hid in the stairwell; the conversation that Bessie and I shared over the pieces of apple pie and tea; how I'd found Papa's Bible with the note in it, and then accepting Jesus as my Savior while kneeling on the floor of Bessie's bedroom.

"Do you know that that makes us sisters?" she asked with a smile.

"Sisters?"

"Yes! We are sisters in Christ," she said. "When you accept Jesus as your Lord, you become a sister to others who have accepted Him as well, and they become your brothers and sisters in Christ."

I could feel hot tears begin to well up in my eyes. Sisters. I had a sister for the first time in my life. I was no longer alone in this world. Violet wisely allowed me to sit and reflect, turning her attention to the mud-flaked window to watch the small towns and farms quickly rush past us.

Eventually, the conductor passed through our train car, announcing that we would soon be arriving in St. Louis. We kept our bare toes hidden underneath our long skirts, and once he had disappeared into another car, we quickly pulled on our stockings and shoes.

Before long, the town of St. Louis rushed into view, and as we gazed out the window, Violet pointed out familiar landmarks. The train began to slow, jolting us occasionally, and Violet held little Nicole tightly to keep her from tumbling onto the floor.

The St. Louis station appeared, and the train sent thick, white steam rushing across the crowded platform, obscuring everything from view. When it did, Violet turned to me and gently held my hand. "Grace, are you sure that you want to travel further west? We could help you, if you wanted to stay here."

I thought about it for a few seconds but shook my head. "No. I think that this is something that I need to do – something that I need to do for me."

Her smile was sad, but she nodded her head that she understood, then pressed a small piece of paper into my hand. "This is my address. Please write to me! I promise that I will be praying for you, Grace."

I nodded gratefully and hoped that I had made the right decision. The steam cleared, and Nicole was the first to spot her parents waiting on the platform. "Mamma! Papa!" she squealed, waving frantically. They caught sight of her and began to wave back, laughing at her excited antics.

We gathered our bags and slowly made our way down the aisle to the steps. The conductor was waiting patiently for us with the step stool already in place. He took our baggage first and reached a sturdy hand out to assist us. Violet and Nicole were the first to depart.

"Mamma! Papa!" Nicole squealed again, as she struggled to free herself from the conductor's strong hands. She made short work of it and rushed head-long into her mother's open arms. Violet made her way quickly down the steps as well, glad to finally be home at long last. The conductor reached out and steadied me by my elbow as I eased my way down until I was safely on the station platform. Even in the excitement, Violet remembered me. She walked back to where I stood, firmly grasped my arm, and led me over to meet her friend, Rebecca.

"Rebecca, I must introduce a new friend to you. This is Grace Ferrell. She kept us company all the way from New York. It would have seemed such a long trip if we had not met her!" she exclaimed, smiling.

Rebecca smiled graciously. She had the most beautiful auburn hair, stunning gray eyes, and a very warm smile. Like Violet, there was something magnetic about her as well.

"Thank you for being such a good friend to Violet and Nicole," she said warmly. "It's such a long trip from New York. I always worry about them, but it gives Nicole the opportunity to visit with her grandmother and Violet the chance to see her mother." She turned to the tall, dark-haired gentleman standing quietly beside her. "Tom, I would like you to meet Grace. She kept Violet and Nicole company on the train."

"Will you be here in St. Louis for long?" he asked cordially.

"No. I'm afraid that I will be buying a ticket to Marshall and will be continuing," I responded. "I'm planning to stake a claim under the Homestead Act."

Although his thick, dark eyebrows arched upward in surprise, he made no comment. I suppose he decided not to argue about the sanity of a decision with a stranger.

"Well, thank you for looking after Violet and Nicole, and good luck on your trip!" He began to slowly herd his group toward an awaiting buggy.

Violet turned around quickly. "Don't forget me," she shouted over the loud din of the train station's noise. "Please write!"

She waved goodbye and finally stepped up into their buggy. The driver whistled to his dappled gray team, and the buggy lurched forward, taking the family with it. I watched until they vanished from view into the helter-skelter of city traffic.

I purchased my ticket to Marshall, but since the train would not arrive for several hours, I decided to explore St. Louis alone. It appeared to be a very modern town with brick-paved streets, fancy restaurants, and shops lining the district. As I stepped out from the train station's lobby into the bright spring afternoon, I decided to venture left and walked briskly down the bustling, paved sidewalk to stretch the kinks from my aching muscles. I stopped and looked intently into the windows of gaily decorated shops, eyeing some of the latest fashions from New York and Paris. With a pang of regret, I reminded myself that this was not a shopping trip and that I needed to dearly conserve my money. I could only imagine how much a wagon and team would cost me, and I knew that there would be many other things I would have to purchase for the long trip.

I did, however, stop at a hat shop that had a bright green and white awning that arched over the sidewalk. I was gazing intently into the window when I spied *the* hat. It was a small, smart-looking black hat with soft netting. It would not take up too much room, I convinced myself, and I needed something desperately to boost my sagging spirits now that I was traveling alone. Taking a deep, determined breath, I quickly opened the door and walked into the refreshing coolness of the shop.

"May I help you?" One of the shop's ladies approached me with a smile.

She was a few years older than me, dressed in simple working-class attire: a modest gray dress with a high collar and her brown hair pulled up tightly into a conservative bun.

"Yes," I replied, "I would like to try on that small black hat in the window."

She graciously seated me at a mirrored vanity, then excused herself to retrieve the hat. Within a few moments, she returned with it and pinned it securely into place. I played with the netting until it draped teasingly over one eye, then tossed my head saucily, observing the effect it gave in the large mirror before me. "I'll take it!" I exclaimed and paid the hat's handsome sum with little regret.

Back out onto the paved sidewalk, I shaded my eyes with my hand and gazed intently up and down both sides of the street. Smart-looking black buggies with shoppers and newly painted supply wagons wove chaotically up and down the shopping district streets. It would be difficult, and perhaps dangerous, to cross the street here. Having spied nothing else that caught my fancy anyway, I continued my present course.

   I found a quaint bookshop whose display window had small children's books dangling from silky-colored ribbons of various lengths. With the late afternoon sun baking down on me and my travel bag feeling much too heavy for my arm, I decided to step inside and browse. A tiny bell tinkled from the top of the entrance door, announcing to the proprietor that he had a customer. The cool, dim room began to immediately refresh me. I set the heavy bag down to rest my weary limbs and began to intently scan the rows of books that had been neatly placed in oak, white-washed bookcases. The proprietor was a gentleman of short stature with strands of dark hair combed across his head to hide a thinning hairline. He wore a limp, white shirt and dark pants with black suspenders – a suitable outfit for unpacking heavy boxes of books.

   "May I help you?" he asked quite cordially as he walked toward the front counter.

   "I'm looking for something to read on the train," I explained. My voice trailed off as I intently scanned the rows of books in search of a compelling title. He stood quietly behind the counter, awaiting my selection. I must have become so engrossed in searching for a book that I lost track of time. When I finally found one that I wished to

A Sister and a Hat

purchase, he had resumed his previous chore behind the bookcases.

I sighed deeply and picked up the gray leather bag. My arms ached terribly. It would be good to sit and rest for a bit. A deep, complaining rumble radiated from my stomach. I had not eaten properly since the evening I left home. Since my departure, my diet had consisted of a few pieces of fruit and sweet bread – nothing that would strengthen someone who wished to travel westward into the wilderness!

I gently tapped the small silver bell that sat on the front counter to summon the proprietor. The gentleman soon appeared attired in a crisp change of clothing. His hair was neatly combed into place, and I could detect the faint smell of inexpensive toilet water.

"Have you found a selection?" he asked politely, with a wide smile.

"Yes, I certainly have," I responded cordially. I placed the book carefully on the counter, opened my bag, and looked up expectantly, awaiting the book's total.

"That'll be five cents." He appeared to look at me with great interest.

I carefully reached into my bag and brought out a five-cent piece.

"Will you be taking your evening meal here in St. Louis?" he inquired slowly, carefully measuring his words as he spoke.

"Yes," I responded with a distant smile, "but it shall be a brief one, and then I'll be leaving." Quickly gathering my things, I bid him a polite but crisp farewell. With a brief, backward glance, I closed the door of the shop. The proprietor stood behind the counter watching, looking very disappointed.

Dusk was about to overtake me when I stepped outside of the small bookshop. It would not be wise of me to be wandering about St. Louis on my own in the dark. With several hours still left to bide, I began to hastily retreat in the direction I had come from.

St. Louis had taken on a new look. Soft light from oil lamps radiated from the store buildings as employees quickly busied themselves to finish their daily tasks. A gentleman in a black cap and overalls walked carefully down the street on long wooden stilts. He paused briefly to light the tall gas lamp beside me and slowly lumbered on to the next.

The streets had become more amicable with the close of business hours. Buggies continued to travel up and down the street but were at a much slower pace. My own energy was quickly waning as well. With each step, my bag became heavier and closer to the sidewalk, and my aching arm began to sadly fail me. I would have to stop soon to rest, so I began to scan both sides of the street for a suitable restaurant.

I soon spied one on the opposite side of the road. Its soft gas lights made it appear out of the rapidly approaching darkness. I'd briefly noticed it earlier in the day but had not given it much thought at that time. This evening, it appeared

A Sister and a Hat

a haven for a travel-weary woman. Carefully pacing my step – quickly one moment, then a snail's pace the next – I navigated my way across the street, avoiding oncoming buggy traffic.

   The restaurant boasted fine linen tablecloths and upholstered chairs, a few of which had been placed just outside on the sidewalk for the ambiance. I was glad for the opportunity to rest my weary bones, and I plopped myself immediately into one of the chairs with an "umph!" I was too tired to care whether I appeared genteel or not. Immediately, a young server wearing the typical white shirt-black trouser uniform trotted out to take my order.

   "Good evening, Ma'am, my name is Robert, and I will be serving you this evening. Our special is a roast stew with baby potatoes, carrots, and onions. Would you like to see a menu," he asked.

   "No," I responded quickly, "that actually sounds wonderful." He poured me a refreshing glass of water and trotted back into the building.

   When my food arrived, I realized how famished I was and consumed it without even a glance around me. Afterward, I sat quietly sipping hot tea, enjoying my gluttony. After a bit, it became obvious that the young waiter was ready for me to move on. He began to inquire about my needs every few minutes, so I placed the coins for my meal and his tip on the table, then picked up my heavy bag and regretfully resumed my walk.

   I was careful to walk in the light of the gas lamps and to

avoid any strange-looking men who were walking by themselves along the sidewalk, too. I breathed a deep sigh of relief when I finally made my way back into the safety of the well-lit station. I decided to locate a quiet bench to rest on and stay there until it was time to board the train. It took some time to locate where I would catch it, but after I had been successful, I slipped gratefully down onto a cool, wrought-iron bench. With a deep sigh of relief, I took a short, much-needed nap.

Sometime later, a sudden rush of activity startled me awake. There were people speaking in excited voices throughout the station; although in my still-dazed stupor, I was unable to make out what any of them were saying. A small newsboy dashed by, and I was able to get his attention by shouting out: "What's going on?"

"It's Mr. Lincoln," he shouted back in wide-eyed wonder. "President Lincoln has been shot!"

Five

Welcome to Marshall!

Let us hold unswervingly to the hope we profess, for he who promised is faithful. Hebrews 10:23

    The entire world appeared surreal that evening. People walked by, speaking anxiously about the event. We had heard it first, as the news had been disbursed by telegraph to the train stations. He had been shot while watching a play at Ford Theater.

    The train finally arrived, sending out great billows of white steam, which caused those of us waiting to board momentarily disappear. Marshall was just a few hours train ride from St. Louis, and those in the ladies' car spent the late hour resting. I dozed fitfully off and on, dreaming senselessly about assassinations and wagon trains until the conductor's booming voice awakened me the next morning with a start.

    "Marshall! Next stop Marshall!"

    I sat up quickly and looked through the closed, soot-laden window. There were very few buildings to be seen. Farmhouses were scattered about, here and there – but there was no comparison to the civilization of modern St. Louis. The train began to intermittently jolt us as it began to slow for the station. Heavy iron wheels groaned and squealed on the track until we finally rolled to a complete stop with a final, sharp lurch. The conductor stepped back into the ladies' car and walked quickly down the aisle to assist us as we departed the train. "Welcome to Marshall!" he exclaimed.

The Marshall station was much smaller than I expected. It consisted of a small, unpainted clapboard building and platform. There was not a station manager to be seen. The realization struck me that I was now truly on my own. After judiciously making my way down the platform steps to Marshall's miry road, I began the short trek toward the buildings that comprised the small, primitive town. The buildings and sidewalks were all made of rough-hewn wood as if they had been thrown together in haste to meet the needs of a town that had appeared overnight.

A weathered, unpainted wagon and a team of brown, disheveled horses rolled past, depositing splatters of mud on my skirt. Those who were traversing the mire as well, and others on the wooden sidewalk, appeared not to notice the inconvenience. Numerous men, and women with children in tow, were busy going about their day, entering and exiting the simple shops which lined either side of the town's main road.

I thought it best to locate a place for me to stay first, so I shook the mud from my skirt and smoothed my hair, then followed two simply dressed women into one of the shops. Both ladies were dressed very similarly: cotton dresses with bonnets and dark leather lace-up boots. In contrast, I was dressed in a fashionable green frock, high-top leather shoes

Welcome to Marshall!

with small brass buckles, and my new black hat with veil. I looked very out of place. Even my fair skin was in sharp contrast to their brown, sun-kissed faces, but they seemed genuinely happy as they sorted through the eggs and produce in the mercantile.

I stood just inside the door and examined the building and its contents. It consisted of a single room filled with a variety of goods and a large storage room in the back. Various baskets of all sizes and shapes, festooned with brightly colored yarns and grasses, hung gaily from the rafters above me. Wooden tables, which were placed conveniently about the room, held local produce, eggs, and colorful bolts of practical fabric, very similar to the dresses the women wore. One corner of the store appeared to be devoted to nails, shovels, and the like, and an entire wall was devoted to wagon harnesses and bridles, which hung on wooden pegs. Behind the counter, where the one and only store clerk stood, were simple wooden shelves that held medicinal-type bottles of various shapes and sizes.

I smoothed the skirt of my green dress and ran my fingers over the dress's brocade collar to ensure that it stood properly before approaching the ladies. "Pardon me," I interrupted, "I've just arrived in town and am looking for a suitable place to stay. Would you kindly give me directions to the closest hotel accommodations?"

The women ceased talking and looked at me as if I were an oddity. "There is the Hudson Hotel down the street on the left," one of the women replied. She glanced briefly at her companion and then back at me.

"Thank you very much." I smiled with a polite nod. As I turned and walked out of the primitive shop, I thought that I heard them giggle, and I wondered if it was about me.

The walk to the hotel was not totally unpleasant. I enjoyed the quiet admiration given by the gentlemen whom I passed by on the sidewalk. They tipped dusty, well-worn hats and smiled; and most of the women who were out and about appeared to be friendly, as well. Almost without exception, the women were either carrying babies, or had small children in tow. Some of the women appeared to be very young mothers, and I noticed that a few had several children, each child only slightly older than the next.

The hotel was easy to find – it was the only two-story building on the block. Simple white square columns and rails curved neatly around the establishment's large, inviting porch. Several rocking chairs and a long bench were in use by hotel guests as they chatted amongst themselves. With a firm grip on my travel bag and my chin held high, I walked across the porch and into the hotel lobby, hoping that I would convey a worldly confidence.

For the small town that it was, Marshall's hotel lobby was likely considered grand. It had clean, wooden floors with large, colorful carpets. There appeared to be a tastefully furnished parlor beyond where I stood. A middle-aged gentleman stood attentively behind the front desk. He was dressed in a starched white shirt, black pants, and a small, black bowtie. A mop of thick, jet-black hair was

Welcome to Marshall!

combed neatly back across his head. As I approached the front desk, his wide smile was friendly and warm.

"May I help you, Ma'am?" He turned the guest book around for me to sign. "What type of accommodations would you require, and how long might you plan to grace our beautiful town," he inquired.

"I would like a room, please," I stated with crisp politeness. "I'm not sure how long I will be staying."

"Yes, Ma'am." He held a pen out for me to sign the Guest Register. "Will you be joined by anyone?"

"No. No, I will not," I replied coolly, "but I would like a nice room with a view." I signed my name, Miss Grace Ferrell, in the large guest book, and the hotel's clerk showed me to my room upstairs.

It was a very pleasant room, although not elaborately furnished. Sheer white curtains ruffled in the pleasant breeze that puffed through two sunny, open windows. Next to the windows, there was a small washstand with a pitcher and bowl for washing oneself. An oak rocking chair with a cushion had a tall oil lamp beside it, which looked adequate for reading. A white iron bed with a brightly colored quilt and clean, crisp linens had been furnished for sleeping. I felt very satisfied with myself. Here I am, I thought, independent, doing as I please. What could be better?

After freshening up a bit at the wash basin, I opened my bag and hung my dresses on a brass hook on the back of the door. Alone for the first time in days, my eyelids suddenly felt very heavy, and I was unable to suppress a wide yawn.

It took only a few moments to unbutton my dress and let it slip onto the floor before climbing into the clean, freshly scented sheets. My journey thus far had been exhausting, and it wasn't long before I was sleeping soundly despite the noise of wagons and people hustling about below my bedroom window.

Either I had become fully rested, or something stirred me, but it was afternoon when my eyes opened, and I lay in a half-stupor, listening to the activity outside. I stretched all four limbs widely, enjoying the crisp bed linens and the goose-down mattress. I felt compelled to make my bed because I'd always had a servant do it for me. It took little effort to arrange the sheets, pillow, and quilt to my satisfaction, and I thought how proud Ella and Bessie would be to see it.

I chose my blue lace dress, which had tiny white pearls about the rounded neck and on the cuffs of the large, puffed sleeves. Thin Irish lace had been sewn around the bottom of the extra-full skirt, making it look like my petticoat was shyly peeking out from underneath. It slipped easily over my head, but a problem arose when I realized it would not be easy to reach the buttons on the back without assistance. The job made it necessary to reach behind and twist around until I located each button and the hole it was intended to inhabit. By the time I'd succeeded, the task left me quite breathless. After washing the remnant of sleep from my face and tidying my hair, I decided to venture out into the town of Marshall. My precious dowry and mother's jewelry also

Welcome to Marshall!

went, tucked securely under my arm in a handbag.

"Would you please tell me where City Hall is located?" I inquired of the clerk once I'd reached the lobby.

He smiled at my request. "Well, Ma'am, this is a small town, and we don't have a City Hall. We do have a mayor, though. He has a desk in the Sheriff's Office, right down the street, to your left."

"Thank you." I turned on my heel and walked briskly out of the hotel in search of Marshall's Sheriff's Office.

Just as the clerk had instructed, it was straight down the street from the hotel. A small bell above the door heralded my arrival as I stepped into the spacious room. A stocky gentleman was sitting behind a desk but stood as I entered. "May I help you?" he inquired.

"I'd like to speak to the mayor if he's available," I explained.

"That would be me. Would you have a seat?" He motioned to a chair in front of his desk and, once I had availed myself of it, eased back into his own. He was an older gentleman with dark hair that had begun to display gray streaks at the temples and a thin mustache that curled fashionably at the ends. He was well-attired in a white, starched shirt with a vest and dark pants with a tidy crease. The gold chain to his pocket watch peeked smartly from his vest pocket.

"What can I do for you today?" he asked.

"I'd like to book passage or to join a wagon train heading west," I explained. "I hope to obtain land through the

Homestead Act. Do you know where I might find one?"

The bell on the door announced the arrival of others, and a rough-looking group of men with heavy boots and mud-spattered clothing sauntered in, wearily plunking themselves into chairs that were scattered about the room. Each one had a metal badge pinned onto the left side of a brown leather vest. All eyes were curiously on me.

The springs on the mayor's chair complained with a groan as he leaned back in contemplation. He made a tent out of his fingers and placed them against his thin, chapped lips, deep in thought. "You by yourself?"

"Just me," I smiled back. Two of the men chuckled in amusement. I felt small and foolish.

The mayor leaned forward, making the springs of his chair complain once more. "Ma'am, my advice to you is to go back home. It's a very dangerous trip. People die out there. This is not the type of trip that a fine lady like yourself can make on her own."

"Nonetheless, I would like to speak to the wagon master myself," I responded unflinchingly. "I have not come this far on my own to turn back around. Where might I find him?" I stood from the chair. My cheeks began to feel warm again. Turn back? To go where?

The mayor eased back into his wooden chair once more, shaking his head with a deep sigh. "If you insist, you can find him down by his lake camp. He has a group that he plans to take west next Monday, but I doubt that he will take you, and even if he agrees to, I doubt that you could be

Welcome to Marshall!

ready by then."

"And where might that be?" I forced myself to speak calmly.

"If you continue to follow the main street, about three miles out of town, you will come to a pasture area and a lake. That is where he and all of the folks he is taking are gathering."

"You'd best stop by the livery stable and rent yourself a buggy," a tall, lanky man advised from across the room. His badge indicated that he was the town's sheriff. "It's farther than you think if you're not used to walking, and it might be getting dark by the time you head back to town. It wouldn't do for you to be out walking around by yourself after dark. Sometimes these cowpokes that pass through get to drink'n and don't have any regard for anybody," he warned.

"Thank you. Yes, I will," I nodded in appreciation. "Thank you, sir." I acknowledged the mayor. I picked up my bag and took my leave, but I heard them speak to each other before the door closed completely behind me.

"She's a spunky one," the sheriff commented across the room to the mayor.

"Yeah, too bad she's come all this way for noth'n," he replied with a sigh.

Six

The Wagon Master

This is my commandment, that you love one another as I have loved you. John 15:12

Just as the sheriff had advised, I made my way to the livery stable to obtain a horse and buggy. "Hello?" I called into the barn. A tall young man with dark, curly hair stepped out of a stall and into the barn's center aisle.

"Can I help you?" he asked. He picked up a rag and wiped his soiled hands.

"I'd like to rent a buggy for a short time," I explained. "I just need to drive out to the lake and back." He looked at me and gave me a charming, lopsided smile.

"Can you drive yourself?" he asked. "I'm the only one here right now, so I can't leave the barn."

I smiled back. "No, but I'm a quick learner. I've watched plenty of other people drive. If you give me a few pointers, I bet I can drive myself."

He smirked, and his eyebrows lifted as he sized me up. "I'll make a deal with you. I'll give you a quick lesson; you show me around here that you can handle it, and then you must promise you won't run over anyone."

I smiled back and nodded in agreement. The young man pulled out a small black buggy with a bench seat and wiped it down with a clean cloth until it shined. Afterward, he thoroughly groomed a small black mare before placing her in a buggy harness. "This is Lady. She's the gentlest horse we have here. She'll take good care of you," he promised.

After Lady was hitched to the buggy, he climbed onto the seat and motioned for me to join him.

"You hold the reins like this," he instructed. "You're going to kiss at her and flop the reins gently on her back. She'll start walking straight. When you want to go left, you pull gently on the left rein until she turns. When you want to go right, you pull gently on the right rein until she turns right. When you want to stop, you say *woah*, pull back gently, and ease up as soon as she stops. When you stop, you pull this handle back. It's the brake. When you are ready to leave, you release it like this." He demonstrated the brake for me, then said, "It's very simple to drive her. She's very sweet, so be nice to her."

He handed the reins over, and I drove around the livery yard with him sitting beside me until he was satisfied; then, he climbed down from the buggy and placed his hands on the reins. "Repeat after me," he instructed, with a feigned serious expression. "I promise not to run over anyone."

"I promise," I repeated.

The drive to the lake was pleasant, and just as the young man had said, Lady was indeed true to her name. She jogged along happily as if she knew the way, and before long, we approached a cluster of white canopied wagons gathered about a large, grassy lake area.

Several oxen, horses, and cows grazed contentedly on

the lush, green pasture grass, and groups of white, red, and black chickens scratched about for bugs under and about the wagons. Small, barefoot children of various ages raced around, laughing and playing tag with each other, while women dressed in simple cotton dresses and bonnets busied themselves doing laundry by the lake. I could see several men stoking campfires and salting fresh meat while others appeared to be making repairs on harnesses. My guess was that the wagon master would be in the white military-type tent, which had been pitched in an area away from the main group. I drove Lady underneath the shade of a nearby tree, set the brake, and climbed down.

The flaps of the tent were pulled back, and three men sat inside. One muscular gentleman with thick gray hair and a mustache sat at a makeshift table studying a map. The other two, both younger and smaller in stature, leaned lazily back in chairs – their feet propped against the table, with wide-brimmed hats pulled over their eyes.

"Excuse me," I said as I stood outside the tent, looking in at them. "Is this where I can find the wagon master?"

"Yes, ma'am," the gentleman with the gray mustache replied. "You have found him." He stood and offered me his chair. "What can I do for you?" The two younger men, startled to hear a woman's voice, quickly took their feet off the table and placed their hats appropriately on their heads.

"I am interested in joining your wagon train going west next Monday," I replied. "Would you have room for another?"

"Yes, ma'am, we have room for another wagon," he said. "How many will be in your party?"

"Party?" I knew where he might be going with the conversation and was not going to back away without a fight.

"Yes, ma'am. Will you be traveling with your husband and children, brother or father? You know . . . who all will be in your wagon is what I mean." He smiled, and the edges of his mustache curled upward with the sides of his mouth.

"Just me." I smiled back.

The two younger men sat quiet and still, listening intently. "Oh, ma'am," the wagon master apologized with a sad smile. "I am sorry, but we just don't take unaccompanied ladies. It would be impossible for the men to care for your animals and wagon and their own stock too. There have been a few women and children who made the trip alone, but these were tough women who were used to the type of hardships that we'll face on the trail. This is a very hard journey, even under the best of conditions. I'm sorry that we can't help you." He shook his head sympathetically. "Whatever your situation is, it can't be that bad. Ma'am, go back home," he urged. With that, he gently lifted my elbow to remove me from his seat and escorted me to the doorway of the tent.

"What if I could get one of the families to allow me to travel with them?" I inquired.

"If you can get someone to agree to let you travel with them, then that would be all right. . . but you cannot bring a wagon of your own. We just couldn't handle the extra work," he said. This time his voice sounded a bit stern.

"Thank you, Sir," I said with a smile. I slowly backed out of the tent and headed eagerly for the wagons.

The mid-afternoon sun felt warm against my face as I trudged across the thick, green carpet beneath me toward the scattered encampment of white-canopied wagons. The sweet scent of clover caught in the light spring breeze and the excitement I felt about the westward journey made me feel a bit heady. Even the cow paddies and horse dung, of which I had to navigate, could not dampen my excitement.

I cautiously approached the closest wagon, where a slightly balding man sat on a short, three-legged stool. He whistled softly to himself, intent on the repair of a harness. A large brown dog with long ears sprawled lazily at his feet, napping soundly in the warm afternoon sun.

"Excuse me, sir." I approached cautiously, unsure how the dog would react to a stranger. "Could I trouble you for a minute?"

"Yes, ma'am?" he said with a slight scowl. He ceased his work and looked up. "What can I do for you?"

"I am looking to book passage on a wagon heading west. Would you be interested in taking a passenger this Monday?" I anxiously attempted a friendly smile.

"Booking passage?" he snapped surly. "Ma'am, I couldn't possibly take anyone else. We haven't even started, and already I'm having trouble," he grumbled. "No, I just can't handle anything else." He began mumbling to himself as he returned to his harness work, quickly dismissing me.

"Well, thank you anyway, sir," I sighed. Feeling somewhat disheartened, I carefully stepped over the tongue of his large wagon and walked toward the next site.

This time, I found a pleasant young woman with a shock of braided red hair and a sprinkle of light brown freckles across her slightly upturned nose. She had a small child playing at her feet and a slightly rounded tummy. Her attention was divided equally between the busy child and a butter churn that she steadied securely between her knees. As I approached, she looked up and smiled, and my heart lit up to see a friendly face – someone whom I could visit with, if only for a few moments.

"Hello!" She smiled at me from her work. "That's a mighty fine dress you are wearing," she noted. "You must not be from around here."

"No, I'm not," I admitted, "which seems to be very obvious to everyone!"

The little boy stood up and toddled toward me with a muddy stick in his chubby hands. He grabbed onto the skirt of my dress to steady himself, then held up the stick, smiling.

"He is giving you a present," the young woman said with a lighthearted laugh and an apologetic smile. " I hope that he didn't dirty your dress too much."

"Oh, not at all," I replied, trying to hide a grimace. I leaned down to accept the stick from the little boy's hand.

"Would you like to sit for a spell?" she asked, "There's

another stool in the back of the wagon if you'd like."

"Yes, thank you. I think that I would." I admitted.

Inside their wagon everything which could be, was tied neatly to the canopy ribs: buckets, pots and pans, and canvas sacks jutting with personal possessions. There were blankets rolled up, a few pillows; some clothes hung on a white cord strung across the wagon's ribs. A large kettle and an old, weathered plow were securely lashed to the side with rope.

Just as she'd said, I spotted the stool at the back of the wagon next to four large wooden barrels. What a simple life they must live, and I remembered my own travel bag, which held just a few precious possessions. With the stool in hand, I joined the young woman and sat.

"My name is Anne. What's yours?" She asked without any shyness.

"Grace." I shifted around on the wooden seat. The stool was so low to the ground that it was nearly impossible to look lady-like sitting on it.

"What brings you out here?" She busied herself, pumping the long handle of the butter churn.

"I'm looking for a way to travel west when the wagon train leaves next Monday. The wagon master said that I could go if I could find a family that would let me travel with them," I admitted.

"And you were wanting to know if we would let you travel with us?"

I took a deep breath. It didn't seem likely. "Yes," I

confessed, unable to keep a sad smile from creeping across my face.

She looked sad for me, too. It made me feel worse than I already did. "It would be so nice to have company and help with little Samuel here and the new one on the way . . . but my Jesse, he likes our privacy. We've only been married, less than three years now, and I guess we're like newlyweds still," she smiled.

"I understand." I nodded my head and forced a smile. I wished that for myself: someone who would love me, too. She looked so happy and content with her simple life, her husband, and babies, something, perhaps, that I might never know. After cordially thanking her for her hospitality, I placed the stool back in the wagon and continued.

A well-rounded woman with thick brown hair wound neatly into a bun walked breathlessly toward their wagon. She was struggling to keep a large armload of freshly dried laundry from spilling onto the ground. A small, brown-haired boy jogged quickly behind, carrying a few towels in his arms. She smiled warmly at me as I strolled toward them.

"May I help you with that?" I offered. I had never carried laundry before. My heart pinged with the pitiful recollection of my former life, and I felt useless.

"Why, yes," she smiled. She carefully divided her laundry, handing me half of the load. "That's a lovely dress," she commented. "You don't look like you are from around here. My name is Claudia."

"My name is Grace," I replied. We made our way back toward her wagon with the laundry and a little boy in tow.

"This is my youngest, Luke." She smiled proudly at the little boy, then placed her pile of laundry on a table beside their wagon. I quickly followed suit. "What brings you here to our campsite?" She reached down and took the towels from little Luke's chubby hands and gave his forehead a rewarding kiss.

"I'm looking for a family who'll allow me to travel with them when you leave this Monday. I thought that perhaps I could be quite a bit of help to someone: caring for children, cooking, or doing laundry." Of course, I had never done any of those things before. Claudia looked thoughtful as she began to smooth and fold her laundry. I was encouraged that she had not said no yet, so I began to follow her example, but not quite as well. She looked at me curiously and with some amusement as I fumbled about.

"You've never done laundry before, have you?" She chuckled as she watched me wrinkle her clothes. I grimaced and stopped my efforts.

"No," I answered honestly. "Am I that awful? Is it that obvious?"

"Oh, honey," she said with an understanding smile and good-natured laugh. "Everybody must learn from somebody. My guess, by looking at you, is that someone has always done everything for you. Am I right?"

"Yes, I hate to admit that you're right." I smiled, although I felt another painful jab in my heart. It was a struggle not to allow my eyes to tear up, and I pinched myself under the table to prevent it.

"This would be a terrible time to learn how to be domestic!" she exclaimed, shaking her head. "This is going to be a very hard trip. Look around you," she said as she pointed around the pasture to the people busy working and the little barefoot children playing. "Chances are that some of these people are not going to make it. Some of them may decide to turn back around and go home, and some may even die and be buried out there on the trail. Why would someone like you decide to do something like this?"

It had become a very disappointing day, and before I could stop it, a flood of tears gushed out of my eyes. I sobbed at Claudia's table and on her clean laundry. She let me pour my heart out to her, and I was terribly grateful for it, holding nothing back. She looked exhausted at the end of my story but gave me a warm, comforting hug, just like I imagined Mama would do if she were here.

"Well, Grace, if I had room, I'd be glad to let you travel with us. Lord knows I could sure use some help around here with seven children," she said. She brushed soft wisps of brown hair from her face and picked up little Luke into her soft, fleshy arms. "Let me tell you who's going, point out their wagon, and you can decide what to do. All right?"

I nodded gratefully and wiped the tears from my face with one of her crisp, white towels.

She pointed to the first wagon that I had inquired about. "That is Mr. Wilbur and Lydia Biggs. She is *really* nice. He is grumpy. They are traveling with her mother, who complains about everything. They don't have any children. This next wagon is Jesse and Anne Smith. They have a little boy, Samuel, and a little one on the way."

"Yes, I met her already," I nodded my head.

"The wagon next to us is Michael and Anita Collins. They have four of the cutest little blond-haired and blue-eyed girls you have ever seen. The wagon on the other side of them is Abraham White, his elderly mother, and his spinster daughter, Mary Beth."

I winced at the word spinster, and Claudia noticed. "Sorry." She smiled apologetically. "I didn't mean anything by it. Then, there is another wagon on the far side of the pasture, which came in last night. They've slept in late today—probably traveled for a while, but I can't say anything about them since nobody has been out and about."

I gave Claudia a grateful hug. It had been wonderful to have someone to unburden myself to. I promised that I would let her know what happened and ventured off through the deep green pasture to the next wagon.

Claudia was right . . . the Collins all had beautiful blonde hair and blue eyes. They looked like a wagon full of cherubic angels, but Mrs. Collins sadly shook her head no.

Mary Beth stood outside their wagon. Although she was considered a spinster, she didn't look much older than I was. Attired in a light pink cotton dress with lace and tiny white buttons up front, she was dressed much nicer than the other women I had already met. Long, silky, raven-colored

The Wagon Master

hair cascaded down her slender back in a loose braid. What a pity that such a beautiful woman was still unattached.

"I'm sorry," she said with a sweet, sympathetic smile. "It would be wonderful to have someone else to talk to – but my grandmother is so demanding. I'm afraid that it would be a really crowded, miserable trip." Just then, a shrill, demanding voice called out from inside the wagon:

"Mary Beth! Mary Beth, come here!"

"I'm sorry, Grace. Good luck," she said with a soft smile and sad-looking eyes. She climbed up into the back of the wagon and disappeared.

I had only one more wagon left to check. Hoping that they would not be angry about the intrusion, I began to walk quickly across the pasture to the last family. By the time I neared their campsite, I noticed that a man had risen and was busy trying to start a fire. His hair was dirty and disheveled, and his face was unshaven. By the odor that crept pungently toward my nose, he hadn't had a bath either in as many days.

I dismissed my first impression of him since I knew that the family had probably traveled quite some distance to be able to leave with the group on Monday. He appeared to notice my approach with interest and sat back on his heels. I cautiously stopped a respectable distance from him.

"Good afternoon," I said, trying to sound cheerful. "Might I have a word with you?"

"Yes, ma'am," he said with some amusement. "What can I do for you today?" He had a casual, friendly smile as he continued to stoke their small, growing fire.

"I'm looking for passage on a wagon heading out this Monday. I'm willing to help with the children, cook, and do laundry. Would it be possible that you could consider it?"

His eyes narrowed, and he stared at me for quite some time, making me feel uncomfortable. Then he smiled. "Yes, of course. We could sure use some help around here. Let me show you where everything is," he said with a grin. "Maybe there are some things that we still need to get before we leave."

"Of course." I agreed with him and tried hard not to breathe too deeply. The first thing that he needed to get was a bath.

There was a large barrel by the wagon, and he began to show me pots and pans as well as sacks of flour and coffee. I stood quietly by, trying to listen intently to everything that he said while blocking out his stench. Without any warning, he turned and tightly gripped the bare part of my shoulder until it hurt; then pinned me against the wagon. Like a babe, I was startled, stunned, and too afraid to move or even speak.

"Come out here and see what I have," he shouted to the inside of the wagon. An equally filthy man jumped out of the back.

"Why, she's real perty." He spit a nasty brown wad of tobacco onto the ground. "Where'd you find her?" he asked.

I flinched as his partner dug his short, jagged nails deeper into the soft flesh of my shoulder. "She's come to

The Wagon Master

help us," he announced with a smile. He moved his greasy, smelly body closer to me, and I closed my eyes tightly. Then I heard the noise: CLICK-CLICK! The man let go of my shoulder, and I opened my eyes to see him back away.

"Miss, you need some help?" Wagon Master and his two young trail hands stood just a short distance away. The two wicked men froze like statues as they stared down the menacing barrel of Wagon Master's long rifle.

Seven

A Dinner Invitation

"A new heart also will I give you, and a new spirit will I put within you: and I will take away the stony heart out of your flesh, and I will give you an heart of flesh." Ezekiel 36:26

The frightening encounter with those two wicked men left me quite shaken. Mr. Wheeler, the wagon master, insisting that I be driven back to the hotel, served as escort on his large bay horse. Jeff, one of his young trail hands, sat next to me in the buggy driving the gentle black mare. His own horse, tied to the back of the rig, trotted quietly behind.

"You won't need to worry about those two, Miss Grace," Jeff said. "Mr. Wheeler is going to talk to the sheriff about them before we leave town this evening."

My mind was numb and cold from the ordeal. I had only wished to make a new life for myself. Perhaps everyone was right. Perhaps I should turn back around and head for . . . where? And to do what?

Jeff drove the buggy up to the hotel steps, set the brake, and ran around to my side to assist me. He seemed a nice young man, with wavy brown hair and brown eyes – and had a distinctive southern accent when he spoke.

"Here, Miss Grace, let me help you." He politely offered me a tan, range-roughened hand. "I'll be glad to take the buggy back to the stable for you."

"Thank you, Jeff," I reached out and took his outstretched hand to steady myself to the ground. While our hands were still clasped, I squeezed his hand briefly in gratitude. Once back on solid ground, I turned my attention to the man astride the large bay. "And thank you, Mr. Wheeler."

"You're welcome, ma'am." He nodded and tipped his wide-brimmed hat briefly forward. "Sorry about the trouble you had. I'll be sure to let the sheriff know about them."

I stood on the hotel porch and watched them ride away: Mr. Wheeler toward the Sheriff's Office and Jeff toward the livery stable. It was truly amazing that these tough, courageous men who battled the elements and the danger of traveling west could be so gentle.

***

The next morning found me sitting once again in the Sheriff's Office in front of the mayor's large oak desk.

"I'm sorry, ma'am, but we already have a school marm." The mayor stretched then leaned way back, and his chair groaned in complaint.

"Are there any positions elsewhere that might be available for someone with my qualifications?" The edge of the straight-back chair bit into the back of my legs, making me shift around.

"No, ma'am." He ran his fingers through his hair and sighed. "We're still a small town, and most of our businesses are owned by families. They usually don't need any help. Of course, you're certainly free to ask around." He leaned forward, and his chair groaned again. "I'm sure sorry that I can't be more help to you."

"Well, thank you, anyway." I stood, took a deep breath, and forced myself to give him a cordial smile. He respectfully stood from his chair and gave a sympathetic nod.

"Good luck to you, Miss."

"Good day, Sir." The wooden heels of my expensive French shoes made sharp, staccato clips as they retreated across the freshly mopped office floor. Once outside on the sidewalk, I squinted my eyes against the brightness of the early afternoon sun and scanned up and down the busy, miry street of Marshall. *There is no place for me*, a small, tormenting voice inside of me whispered; and I struggled to keep a mournful sob from escaping my lips.

To the left and across the street, a small, white-washed building stood out from the plain-faced wooden structures that lined the main street of Marshall. The entrance boasted a pair of arched, double doors with neatly carved crosses in their centers and large brass handles. Above the doors was a round stained-glass window with a dove of peace. In its neat simplicity, the house of worship affirmed a town that treasured its presence. I had not graced the steps of the inside of a church since I'd attended with Mama. We had stopped attending when she became ill and had not again except for her and Papa's funeral. I thought about my new relationship with the Lord and felt a pang of regret that I had not opened the pages of the Bible since I had accepted Christ. Perhaps that's where I was amiss. I had been doing this on my own and had not sought direction from the Almighty. Something in my heart stirred, and feeling the need to seek God's plan for my life, I stepped off the sidewalk and made my way to the church.

It was cool and quiet inside the small building – not at all like the churches that Mama had taken me to. Those had been large and ornate with arching cathedral ceilings, grand, stained-glass windows, and intricately carved pews with soft, velvet cushions.

Apart from the single stained-glass window above the arched doors, this church had simple glass panes for windows and plain cushion-less wooden pews. At the head of the room stood a white wooden podium with a simple cross on the front. There were no special choir lofts from which an angelic-sounding choir of parishioners could sing inspiring hymns. Back then, when I thought of church, I thought of the beautiful building and the music that entertained me; today, however, my thoughts were focused on spiritual things and the relationship I wished to pursue with the Lord. But how to get started? As a child of His, could I just speak to the Creator of the Universe, and He would reply?

"Are you there?" I stood in the center aisle and spoke aloud in the empty room. "I need Your help," I continued. "I didn't think this through very well, and now I don't know what to do. Will you help me?" My pleas were swallowed up by the stark stillness of the room. Silence.

Utter desperation took over, and when the sudden burning of hopeless tears welled up in my eyes, I quickly slid into one of the simple wooden pews next to me and allowed myself to cry. I felt a warm, comforting hand on my shoulder. "God says in the Bible: 'For I know the plans that I have for you . . . plans for peace and not for evil, to give you a future and a hope'."

Startled, I turned around quickly and saw an older man with soft, graying hair sitting in the pew behind me. He had kind, blue eyes and a gentle smile.

"Oh! I'm so sorry!" Embarrassed, I quickly wiped the tears from my eyes. He handed me a clean, white cotton handkerchief. "The door was unlocked," I explained, "so I thought it would be all right to come in. My name is Grace."

"Nice to meet you, Grace. I'm the pastor of this fine church." He smiled, gesturing his hand about as if the building was a grand cathedral. "I'm sorry that I interrupted you, but I would like to help if I could. God is still in the miracle business, but I've been known to assist when I can."

"I think that this is one that God will have to do himself." I struggled to contain another round of tears.

"All right, then let's ask Him to help, and then you can give me a try," he said with a sympathetic smile. With nothing left to lose, I prayed with him. First, he prayed for me, and he prayed for God to give him wisdom; then he made me pray for myself. Afterward, I told him the long story about how I ended up in Marshall: Papa and Angela's

A Dinner Invitation

marriage, Papa's sudden death and his *Will*, Jerrold and Angela, me asking Jesus to be my Savior, and my decision to head out west. "Well, young lady, you certainly are in a pickle," he smiled, "but God is in the pickle-getting business." We were interrupted by a tall, handsome man with sandy-blonde hair. He looked startled and embarrassed to have walked in on us.

"I'm sorry, Father, I didn't know that anyone else was in here." He stammered, and his cheeks flushed red.

"That's quite all right," the pastor said. "I'd like to introduce you to someone, Mark."

The young man smiled and began to walk toward us with long strides. I was pretty sure that he could tell I'd been crying and wished that I could have washed my face.

"Mark, this is Miss Grace Ferrell. She is new to our fine little town."

"Nice to meet you." He awkwardly reached out to briefly take my hand.

"Grace, this is my youngest son, Mark. He assists me here at the church, and we work together to help the congregation members wherever there is a need." He paused for a moment in thought. "Miss Ferrell, I would like for you to be a guest in our home today and for dinner this evening. Meanwhile, I will spend some time in my study, praying and asking God to help me with what we spoke about earlier."

I must have looked hesitant at his offer because he continued. "It would really be our pleasure, and my wife

Molly does so enjoy it when I bring visitors home for her to visit with."

"Why yes, of course," I said, not wishing to offend him; besides, I had nothing else with which to occupy myself.

"That is wonderful!" he exclaimed and slapped the leg of his plain black trousers. "Mark, bring the buggy around. I have a brief errand to run at the telegraph office, and we shall escort Miss Ferrell to our honored home."

***

Molly Peterson made me feel quite at ease. She had the brightest blue eyes, and when she smiled, her face glowed with a youthful exuberance that erased the soft creases of her face. Her thick, blonde hair, which she wore twisted up into a bun, had already begun to discreetly transform into a soft crown of white. Attired in a simple blue dress with a white collar and puffed sleeves, there was an air of quiet elegance about her. After leading me to their guest bedroom, she graciously bade me to treat the room as if it were my own.

"Grace, please feel free to freshen yourself and even take a nap if you'd like. I'm going to spend some time out in my garden." Her smile was kind as she glanced over my wilted hair and drooping eyelids. "You must be exhausted," she said.

I stood aside as she turned down the covers on the bed, revealing clean white linens with ruffled lace edges. "There is clean water in the pitcher if you'd like to freshen up a bit," she motioned toward the matching magnolia-flowered

A Dinner Invitation

pitcher and bowl set, which sat on the room's oak washstand. "You may also feel free to wander the house, but the pastor is in his study, the room with double doors, and he does not like us to disturb him when he closes them. Mark is out back chopping wood. It's one of the ministries of our church: taking care of the women who have been widowed. We keep them supplied with firewood."

I nodded and smiled, grateful for her hospitality. "Thank you for your kindness. Yes, I believe that I would like to freshen up."

"I'll be out in the garden if you need me," she reminded me once again before quietly closing the bedroom door behind her.

Although small, the room was very comfortable. The oak washstand matched the bed's tall headboard and footboard, as did the dresser; and the bed's white quilt had lovely blue tulips with green vines and leaves stitched onto it. There was a small oval blue and white woven rug beside the bed and white ruffled curtains at the window. Outside, I could see a meticulously kept garden that was hedged about with a small, white picket fence and a picturesque grape arbor beyond that.

A gentle rap on the door turned my attention away from the pastoral scene. Mrs. Peterson cracked the door open a bit. "Grace," she said, "It is so warm here today that I thought, since you appear to be about my size, you might like to change into something a little cooler." She held out a simple, but charming pink dress with a sash at the waist.

"Why, Mrs. Peterson, it's lovely!" I exclaimed. "How thoughtful of you! Yes, I would love to wear it if it fits!" She opened the door wider and smiled, pleased. Once she had passed the dress to me, she softly closed the door, leaving me alone once more.

I held the pink frock up to me. It was simple yet fashionable, somewhere between the elegant gowns that I owned and the faded cotton dresses that many of the ladies of Marshall wore. A momentary tug at my heart caused me to pause. I had prayed to God for help, and He had sent it.

It only took a moment to relieve myself of the heavy, dark dress I wore, then kicked it aside with disdain. It had been suitable for early spring back home, but here it was hot and made my skin itch. I'd also grown weary of looking out of place in my surroundings and wished to look the part of a resourceful young woman heading west. How could I expect anyone to take me seriously if I looked otherwise? A quick bath at the washstand with the cool water that Mrs. Peterson had so thoughtfully provided revived me, and taking advantage of a tortoise-shell comb, I took my hair down and made it look as acceptable as possible for my gracious hosts. Mrs. Peterson's pink dress fit me very well, and I was pleased with my appearance when I looked in the mirror. No longer feeling weary from the heat, I decided to take Mrs. Peterson's offer to explore the home.

It was a charming two-story home with clean, white-washed walls and gleaming wooden floors. From the guest room, I stepped into a long hallway; to the left was their

A Dinner Invitation

parlor, and to the right was the kitchen.

The parlor was furnished with a comfortable-looking overstuffed sofa and a chair with a matching ottoman. I could imagine Pastor Peterson sitting in a large chair on a cold winter evening, reading his Bible. His feet would be resting on the ottoman, warming in front of a crackling fire in the fireplace. Mrs. Peterson would be sitting quietly on the couch, reading or doing some needlework. She would stop her work upon occasion and ask Mr. Peterson if he would like some coffee or hot chocolate to warm himself. There was a clock on the mantel of the fireplace with an ornate gold face with fancy roman numerals. It seemed rather out of place with the room's simple furnishings, and I thought, perhaps, that it might be a cherished family heirloom.

A dainty black cat with white paws peeked at me from behind the chair and meowed a soft greeting. "Hello. What is your name?" I asked. She stepped out from her hiding place, and I picked her up. She was very sweet and gentle and began to purr and snuggle into my arms. I couldn't resist brushing my cheek against her soft, warm fur. The two of us continued my tour of the Peterson's home. We quietly passed by the double doors of the pastor's study. I held my breath and tip-toed so as not to disturb him.

Their kitchen was large, with a round table and six straight-back chairs. The table had a crisp-looking blue and white tablecloth and a white milk pitcher filled with vibrant-colored wildflowers in the center. White shelves lined one entire wall, which were filled with colorful dishes and jars of canned goods. A green and blue rug, woven from cotton yard-good scraps, sat below the sink.

    Above the sink was a large picture window, and when Kitty and I leaned over to look out, I could see Mark busy at work. A large pile of wood sat to his left, and an open wagon bed, partially filled with split firewood, to his right. He'd discarded his shirt, and the right strap to his suspender dangled at his waist as he swung the axe to split each piece. Chop-split-toss. Chop-split-toss. Before long, the wagon was nearly full, and I could see heavy drops of perspiration fling from his thick hair with every swing of his body. The volume of work that he'd completed made me realize that I must have been standing there for longer than I'd intended. He suddenly stopped, picked up his discarded shirt, and wiped his face and brow, then turned toward the kitchen window. I gasped, and stepped back from the window, then ventured another peek once I heard the crack of the axe resume its rhythm. A thought occurred to me: I'd been engaged to another man just a few short days ago, and yet here I was, gazing at another man in admiration. Perhaps, Jerrold and I were not meant to be? I was sure that I'd been in love with him, but I had to admit that there seemed something indeed special about the young man who was busy splitting wood for those who needed a helping hand. Jerrold was dashing, well-dressed, and successful, but was also self-absorbed and selfish. I couldn't recall one time that he had ever done something that didn't benefit himself –

even things that seemed charitable. Here was Mark, chopping and splitting wood simply because there was a need. He would receive nothing but their gratitude in return. Jerrold and Mark were two totally different men. I thought about my new-found friend, Violet, from the train. She was different, too. She'd explained that the difference was because she'd accepted Jesus as her Savior; it was then that I realized that I was changing as well. Jesus was changing me. The things that I had been drawn to in the past were no longer important. I was looking at the world with a fresh pair of eyes. I was becoming different. A good different.

Eight

An Unexpected Proposal

The steps of a [godly] man are ordered by the Lord: and he delighteth in his way. Psalm 37:23

"I see that you've found Mittens." Mark allowed the kitchen's screened door to slam behind him as he rubbed his sweaty hair dry with the soiled shirt he'd set aside earlier. He smiled and tossed it into a laundry basket that sat beside the door.

My cheeks flushed pink with embarrassment. I'd allowed my thoughts to take me off guard. Had I been caught spying on the pastor's son? "She is so sweet." I rubbed my cheek against her soft fur, hoping to hide my guilt. She purred louder in response and began kneading my arm with her little white paws.

Mark stepped forward, and our bodies were so close that I could smell his sweat. He reached out and scratched the kitten's head. "Make yourself at home. I believe that my mother is out in her garden. She loves it there." He smiled, then strode out of the kitchen, leaving Mittens and me alone.

Taking his advice, I retreated to the sanctuary of Mrs. Peterson's garden, where I found her on her knees, weeding between rows of tomato plants. "If you would like, Grace, you can help pick some vegetables for our evening meal.

We have a very early garden this year because we started the seeds in containers inside the house," she said proudly.

"Yes, ma'am," I replied. "I'll be glad to help." She seemed pleased that I had joined her and patiently showed me how to pick beans and yellow squash without damaging the vines, then gave me a tour, identifying the various flowers, plants, and vegetables that were growing.

When dinner time neared, she allowed me to help with dinner as well and patiently showed me how to chop vegetables without cutting myself. Mark came back into the kitchen and lit a fire in the stove for his mother. I forced myself to focus on the task at hand: fingers away from the knife, point the tip of the knife down and make a small cut into the squash, then slice. He had washed the sweat from his body and his thick, blonde mane as well. I could smell the freshness of soap made with lemon zest, and I tried to discreetly sniff the air, remembering my earlier shame of being caught spying on him from the kitchen window.

As I busied myself with the task at hand, I couldn't help but wonder if he had stolen glances at me as well and whether there was a young woman somewhere who had made plans for a future with him. Pastor Peterson was absent as we sat down to an evening meal of freshly boiled potatoes, beans, and squash. A bowl of fragrant, hot yeast rolls sat in the middle of the table as well as a small bowl of chilled butter from their root cellar. I watched as Mrs. Peterson and Mark quietly bowed their heads, and I followed their lead. It was Mrs. Peterson who gave thanks.

"Heavenly Father, thank you for this meal that You have provided. Please give the pastor wisdom and boldness as he studies to preach Your word. Thank You for bringing our new friend, Grace, into our lives. In Jesus' name, Amen."

Pastor Peterson emerged from his study toward the end of dinnertime. No one seemed surprised at his late arrival, and as he pulled out his chair from the table, he leaned down and gave the top of Mrs. Peterson's head an affectionate kiss. "Molly, it looks and smells wonderful," he exclaimed. She beamed back at him.

I listened quietly as the family exchanged pleasantries and discussed the details of their day, and I thought about Mama and Papa and our lives together. Papa had been so busy traveling and sitting on the court bench. Mama was busy as well, running the household and donating her time to charitable organizations. We had so much in the way of material things, things that the Petersons didn't have. But with all our abundance, there had always been something missing. My heart ached at their absence. I wished that they could be here at the table with me, watching this family who had so much less than we did, but seemed so happy, nonetheless.

"Molly, that was a delicious meal. Thank you for cooking it." Pastor gave his wife another affectionate peck—this time on the cheek. Then he stood from his chair and turned to me. "Grace, would you mind meeting with me in the study? I have a few things that I wish to discuss."

"Yes, sir," I replied and quickly gathered my plate and

utensils to carry them to the sink. Mrs. Peterson had already filled a dishpan with warm, soapy water, and I regretted that I would be unable to show her my appreciation by doing the dishes in return for their hospitality. As timing would have it, Mark and I reached the sink with our plates at the same time. He smiled and took the plate from me. "Believe it or not, this has been my job since my sisters got married and left home. Mother cooks, and I do the dishes," he smiled. He turned and took one of his mother's colorful aprons from a hook on the wall and tied the sash around his waist. "Don't tell anyone you saw me do this," he teased. "This is how you do dishes manly-style."

Pastor Peterson was waiting for me in his study. It looked just as I imagined it might. He had a large oak desk which was bare except for his well-worn Bible. There were shelves on two walls filled with books of all sizes with various types of covers; some were massive, and others had very few pages. One wall had a large window and a washstand with a pitcher and bowl – perhaps to freshen himself when he became weary. On either side of the study's wide, double doors hung aging portraits in ornate frames. He smiled and stood as I entered, then gestured for me to sit in one of a pair of comfortable but worn tapestry chairs that faced his desk. He stepped to the entrance of the study and called out, "Molly, would you mind accompanying me for a moment?" Then he turned and gave a brief smile.

"I frequently ask Molly to join me in matters. She is very discreet and holds everything in strict confidence that is said in here. The Almighty found the perfect wife for me when He led me to her. I couldn't ask for a more virtuous woman. She puts up with me, after all," he chuckled. "She has no idea what I am going to say, so she'll be hearing everything for the first time, as well."

Mrs. Peterson stepped into the study, and Pastor Peterson motioned her toward the other tapestry chair, then closed the doors before taking his seat once again behind the massive desk.

"Grace," he began, "I contacted a fellow pastor by telegraph today to verify your story – who you are, where you came from, and to inquire as to your character." He reached into the inner pocket of his coat, pulled out a piece of paper, unfolded it, and placed it in front of me on the desk. I glanced down at the words feeling a bit puzzled. "I have a reason that I wanted to be sure that your story was correct, that you were a person of good moral character, and that someone who knew you well could testify on your behalf that they believed you were indeed a child of God – someone who has truly accepted and trusted that Jesus, the Son of God, died on the cross for their sins." I nodded my head, waiting for him to go on. "This pastor checked with the local constable, who knew your family well. He stated that yes, your father was an honorable judge who recently passed away; that you had indeed gone missing, and that you have been an exemplary citizen. He also spoke with Bessie, one of your household staff. He said that she was very relieved to hear that you were all right. She also told him that she had shared verses in the Bible with you and that she was there when you accepted Jesus as your Savior just a short time ago. She said that she wholly believed that you meant it." He paused as if he was measuring the words that he would speak next. I glanced sideways at Mrs. Peterson, who was sitting quietly, looking attentively at her husband, her hands folded in her lap. She has probably heard many things in this room, I surmised.

He continued, "I have been studying the Word this afternoon, spending time in prayer, and this is what I have considered: That you have not asked for any hand-out from the church. That you are looking for assistance in the form of spiritual guidance. Is that correct?" he asked. I nodded my head. I could not go back. They would not allow me to go forward on the wagon train leaving Monday, and my chances of gainful employment in Marshall were slim. Help would need to come from above if it were to come at all. I knew about miracles, although I'd never experienced one myself. If miracles were true, I needed one now. *Lord, I need a miracle.*

"There are three options that have occurred to me while in prayer today: One, we can help you to get back home. You haven't asked for any monetary assistance, but if you are in need, the church is willing to assist you with that. Two, I can vouch for your character, as I know it, and can help you to look for employment here and in some of the surrounding towns". He paused again. "The third option would be that you and Mark could set out together Monday, as husband and wife, and take the gospel with you. You would both be missionaries heading west."

Mrs. Peterson's chair creaked as she leaned forward. Her mouth was slightly open in disbelief. Pastor Peterson continued before she could speak.

"There are several instances in the Bible where God united couples who did not know each other for His glory: There was Esther, who married King Ahasuerus, and she was able to save her people from destruction. There was Rebecca, who married Isaac. They were the parents of Jacob, whom God renamed Israel, and used them to create the Jewish nation and the line that Jesus was born into." He paused briefly. "This is something that you don't have to do, so don't feel pressured to agree to it if you are not one hundred percent sure that you want to. Whatever you decide to do, we will be glad to assist you if we can."

"My father left me a dowery," I admitted, "so I'm not in need of money."

Pastor Peterson looked away and nodded his head as if he were having an internal conversation. "Grace, I'm glad to know that your father saw to your needs before he passed. He must have loved you very much," he paused briefly, contemplating his words before continuing. "Mark has been a hard worker all his life; he's never spent money foolishly and has saved quite a bit. Molly and I have also saved a bit ourselves. We'd be glad to give you and Mark a tidy sum as a wedding gift, and with that and Mark's savings, you'd be well set to purchase your supplies for the trip. Any money from your dowery, once you become a married couple, could help you with things that you might need along the way and to set up your home when you arrive."

    I sat quietly, deep in thought. I was already nearing what some considered a *spinster*, and I remembered with a wince of pain, the two women speaking of it – of me in the seamstress' shop. In just one afternoon, I'd already become quite fond of this family. What if I said *no* to this possible marriage and couldn't find a position of employment? What if there were no future marriage proposals coming my way? And then another thought occurred to me: What if this had been my future all along? What if it was God who led me here, and a life with Mark homesteading in the wilderness and sharing the gospel was my destiny? "What about Mark?" I asked. "What do you think he'd say about it? This is his home and his life," I reasoned, "and he doesn't really know me. Doesn't he have someone here that he is courting or that he is considering?"

    "There has been a girl or two in the past," Pastor Peterson confessed, "but for one reason or another, the courtships didn't last. Perhaps God had a different plan for Mark's life. I believe he has all the qualities to make a good husband and even a good pastor. Up until now, he has been working under my shadow, but I have faith that God will use him. He has been a good son. I took him aside today and spoke to him about it."

    "What did he say?" I inquired. I was now sitting on the edge of my chair, leaning toward the desk. "Since you're speaking to me about it now, he must not have been entirely against it?" I looked again at Mrs. Peterson. She continued to sit quietly with her hands folded in her lap, but the expression on her face spoke volumes. She was afraid that she might lose her son forever.

"I would consider it," I said, "once Mark and I have had the opportunity to discuss it privately." The pastor and I locked gazes.

"Indeed," he said. "Molly, let's take our leave for now." Mrs. Peterson didn't look at me. She quietly stood from her chair and left the room with her husband.

I was left alone in the study to think. Mark seemed a devoted son to his parents. He didn't mind hard work. He was willing to care for others who could not do for themselves: a dedicated, hard-working, caring, charitable person. But was he the type of person who could endure months in the wilderness facing hardship? Adjust to a new wife who might be more of a burden than a blessing – at least in the beginning. Defend our lives?

Pastor Peterson entered the study – this time with his son instead of his wife. "Mark, would you have a seat?" I looked up, and Mark stood in the doorway for a moment – his eyes fixed on me before he took his place in the chair by my side. He seemed as nervous as I felt. Pastor Peterson took his place in front of us, partially sitting on the edge of the desk.

"Well, I've spoken to you both about this prospect – heading west as a couple. This would be an all-or-nothing venture," he explained. "And I suggest that if either of you have any doubt whatsoever, you should not move forward. Grace, we will not allow you to go homeless or starve," he promised, "so don't make this decision based on whether you will or won't be out on the street. Mark, you are a good son and have been my faithful assistant within the church. You've had this afternoon to think about it. To both of you, if you do not feel the Holy Spirit impressing on your heart to go, then don't. I would not want to be encouraging either of you to do anything that is contrary to God's will in your lives. I encourage you to speak honestly and openly about it now. I'm going to leave the two of you to speak privately." And with that statement, the pastor exited the study and closed the door quietly behind him.

We sat in silence for a while – nearly long enough for it to become uncomfortable. I wondered if Mark had decided not to go; not to take me as his wife, and he was searching for the words to say so. A side-long glance at Mark told me that he was indeed nervous. He was grasping the sides of the chair, and his knuckles were white. I decided to let him off the hook.

"I" we turned simultaneously to each other and spoke in unison. It broke the ice, and we laughed anxiously in uncertainty. I faced forward, closed my eyes briefly, and prepared to be rejected by yet another potential groom.

"Grace!" Mark spoke, this time with confidence and authority. I clasped my hands tightly together and turned to face him. This was a new side of Mark that I was facing.

His hair was tousled, his eyes wide in excitement, and he had a mischievous grin on his face. "Grace, I plan to leave Monday with the wagon train. If you'll join me as my wife, we'll share the greatest adventure of our lives!" With each word he spoke, his smile became larger. And he had dimples. His smile was contagious, and I laughed. He stood from his chair and knelt beside mine. I had relaxed my hands, and he reached out and took one in his strong, calloused hand. "What do you say?"

At that moment, I transformed from feeling like a homeless, orphaned beggar to a woman of God receiving an offer of a new life with this young pastor. I gazed into those smiling blue eyes and once again surrendered to the will of God. "Yes!" I proclaimed.

Nine

A Wagon, a Team of Oxen, and an Engagement Ring

I have chosen the way of faithfulness; I have set my heart on your laws. Psalm 119:30

There was much to do before the wagon group left on Monday. Pastor Peterson had a friend, Samuel Wells, who made his livelihood making wagons for those traveling westward. Mark and his father went to see if he had one ready for purchase. We needed a strong team of mules or oxen to pull it, too, that could be used afterward to begin our homestead. Sitting at the kitchen table, I listened to Mark and Pastor Peterson talk about mules, oxen, cows, chickens, roosters, flour, rifles – an entire life, which until a few days ago, I barely knew existed.

Then there was poor Mrs. Peterson. She'd cried after Mark made his decision to leave with the wagon train heading west on Monday. The pastor had insisted that I stay the night since I was 'practically his daughter-in-law.' Lying in bed in the guest room that night, I could hear Mrs. Peterson's sobs and felt very sad that I had caused heartache for such a sweet woman. I could hear the muffled sound of her husband's voice supporting their son's decision.

The next morning when I awoke, Mark and the pastor were gone, and she appeared to have accepted the fact that we would be leaving. Although her eyes were still slightly red from the previous evening's tears, she smiled and began to chat with me about our wedding, which would take place following church services on Sunday, just two days away.

"Grace, you are welcome to wear my wedding dress," she offered graciously. We sat at the kitchen table, making plans over a cup of coffee. "My daughters thought that it was a bit too old-fashioned," she continued, "and they insisted on having their own dresses made. But I have always cherished the idea of passing it down and was a bit disappointed that they didn't want to wear it. Would you like to see it?"

"Yes, I would," I replied with a smile. I'd assumed that on such short notice, I would be wearing an everyday dress for the occasion. It seemed quite a blessing that I would be allowed to borrow her gown.

She led me down to the hall to her and Pastor Peterson's spacious bedroom. It had an ornately carved, mahogany four-poster bed with curtains that could be closed for privacy and warmth. It had several matching furniture pieces: a very large wardrobe, a chest, a vanity, and a washstand. Just like the mantle clock in the parlor, it was out of place in their modest home.

Mrs. Peterson walked over to the wardrobe, swung the doors open wide, and pulled out a white satin and lace gown. It had three-quarter length sleeves, which came to a point below the elbow, and delicate, white lace along the edges. The bodice had tiny pearls sewn in swirling patterns.

A Wagon, a Team of Oxen, and an Engagement Ring

It was breathtaking.

"It's beautiful," I exclaimed.

"Would you like to try it on?" she asked. I nodded my approval.

She assisted me in carefully stepping into the massive skirt. It took both of us to pull it up, and once my arms slipped into the lace sleeves, she adjusted the bodice and carefully buttoned the long row of pearl buttons in the back. Then she reached above the wardrobe and pulled down an ornate French hat box that contained a sweet white hat with soft, white feathers around the crown. I'd seen nothing like it before.

"Sit here," she instructed and patted the bed. Once I was seated, she twisted my hair up, and secured it with hairpins, then placed the hat gently on my head. When I finally stood for inspection, she caught her breath and covered her mouth with her hands.

"Grace! You are so beautiful," she exclaimed. She turned me toward a full-length mirror. "Do you like it?"

I stared at my reflection. It reminded me of my mother's wedding images, and my eyes misted a bit. "I love it, Mrs. Peterson!" I proclaimed and gave her a grateful hug. "Wherever did you find a gown like this?"

"I came from a well-to-do family, too." She said matter-of-factly. My father was not too pleased that I had chosen to marry a young preacher. He said that he had higher aspirations for me." She looked away again and appeared deep in thought.

"Grace, may I ask why you chose to marry Mark? This will be a dangerous, difficult trip, even for those who are accustomed to hardships. If you are unsure, I'm sure that there are many other suitable avenues that we can explore."

It seemed a fair question. She was a mother concerned about her son, who would be going out into the dangerous unknown with a woman that they knew very little of.

"My life was very certain until after my Papa's death, and I accepted the Lord," I began. "It's like that chapter in my life ended, and a new one began. The doors of my old life closed, and there was nothing left for me – not even a home. It seemed as if a new chapter was opening, and it was time to follow that path." I sat back down on the edge of the bed. "Then I met this young woman on the train, Violet, and she spoke about her relationship with the Lord, and I could feel myself grow listening to her testimony. I arrived here and ended up at the church, asking God for His help. Your family and how you live your lives have been an example to me as well. I'd prayed for the Lord's direction and even for a miracle in the pastor's office. It was as if another door had opened for me, and I could feel Him compel me to step through." I could tell that she was listening intently, and the thought of Mark made me smile. "He said our lives would be an adventure." Mrs. Peterson looked at me, puzzled. "Mark said that if I would marry him, our lives would be an adventure," I explained.

Mrs. Peterson reached out and patted my hand. "If you're going to be a pastor's wife," she stated, "it will be an adventure, indeed." A clamor outside drew her to the bedroom window, and she pulled the curtain aside. "Looks like they have you a new wagon and a team of oxen, too. Let's get you out of this dress so that we can go outside and see."

It took longer to unbutton the dress than it did to button it. Mrs. Peterson's fingers trembled anxiously as she struggled to coax the pearl buttons back through the buttonholes. I took deep breaths to remain calm, and we were finally able to slip me out of the massive dress and into the light-weight pink dress Mrs. Peterson lent me. By the time we trotted out of the house together, the pastor and Mark were proudly showing curious neighbors our new purchase. Mark was especially beaming as he patted the muscular neck of one of the large, cream-colored oxen.

"Mark, why don't you show Grace the wheels that will take you to your new home?" Pastor Peterson tactfully announced our presence to his son and those who had gathered to inspect the new purchase.

Mark turned his attention from the handsome team of oxen and the well-wishing neighbors to me. He smiled, and his blue eyes were wide with excitement. The wise pastor began to gently steer the neighbors back home to allow us the opportunity to spend some time alone together.

"Would you like to see it?" Mark reached out and gently took my hand securely in his strong grasp. "Would you like to sit on the seat?"

I stood for a moment contemplating the wagon's large

wheels – apparently, the only route that led to the wagon seat. Mark suddenly let go of my hand, placed both hands securely around my waist, and lifted me upward. I was able to get my left foot on the spoke of the wheel, the right on the wheel rim, and then grabbed onto the side of the seat to pull myself up. As I turned victoriously to invite Mark aboard, he was already scrambling up the side of the wagon.

"Move over, I'm coming up, too!" he shouted. I moved to the opposite side of the seat, and once he was aboard the wagon, he sat beside me.

"Would you like to try it out?" He lifted a long cane pole and handed it to me. "This is what you use to drive the oxen forward. They're driven differently than horses," he explained.

I nodded in agreement, then fumbled a bit with the pole until I had a good grasp of it.

"All right, let's go then," he said.

I could feel my heart race and my cheeks glow pink with excitement. A new adventure! With the creaking of the brake's release and a whistle from Mark, our oxen team leaned forward into their wooden yokes and steadily pulled us out of the Peterson's yard and onto the rutted dirt of the road. Mark reached over, placed his large hand over mine, and touched the wooden pole to the right ox's flank. They slowly lumbered to the left, and the wagon rolled behind them.

"Where are we going?" I asked. A small group of barefoot children, mired in dirt from morning play, trotted

A Wagon, a Team of Oxen, and an Engagement Ring

alongside and began a game of tag. I smiled and waved as they squealed and laughed, ran, and dodged the little boy chasing them. "Not too close," I cautioned as two of the larger boys dared to get dangerously close to the wagon's heavy wheels.

Mark reached into his back pocket and pulled out a folded piece of paper. "We have a list of supplies to get at the store." He unfolded the paper and then studied it briefly. "We can load the wagon right from the store's loading dock. Is there anything missing that you think we might need?"

He reached over and took the long pole from my hands, then passed me the list to look over: four hundred pounds of flour, one hundred pounds of rice and beans, three hundred pounds of bacon, fifteen pounds of coffee, twenty pounds of sugar, twenty pounds of salt, one hundred pounds of grain, seed, soap, a kettle, a frying pan, plates and cups, towels, a tent, a rifle and ammunition, a water barrel, a bucket, a washtub and washboard, rope, and a plow. My eyes went back to the food provisions, and I bit my lip in contemplation. I didn't know how to cook.

The loading dock was located at the back of the general store I had visited just a few days earlier. Mark drove our team and wagon right up to it, then set the brake securely. The store clerk, a tall gentleman with dark, thinning hair and small gold-colored spectacles, trotted eagerly out to greet us.

"Hello, Mark! That's a mighty nice rig. What can I do

for you today?" He was smiling and stood attentively while drying his hands on the thick, green canvas apron he wore. Mark climbed out of the wagon and onto the loading dock, then turned and took my hand to steady me as I stepped onto the platform as well.

"We have a few things that we're going to be needing," he said proudly. He turned to admire our rig and team with the proprietor, then handed him our shopping list. "We're heading west on Monday," he added. "This is Grace, Mr. Jenkins. She's consented to be my bride on Sunday." Both men turned their attention to me.

"Nice to meet you, Miss," the proprietor nodded. "Mark is a fine young man. I've known him since he was knee-high. A fine young man," he repeated. I smiled.

"If you can help me with this list and maybe suggest anything that I might have overlooked, I'd certainly appreciate it," Mark said.

"Yes, sir. You'll certainly need to be well-prepared for a trip like that." The clerk nodded thoughtfully while studying the list, and then he and Mark quickly strode across the loading platform and into the back entrance of the store. I meekly trailed behind. I had no idea what we might need, and it seemed the men had things under control.

Just as I stepped inside, I was swept up by a frail-looking gray-haired woman. She put a thin, heavily freckled arm around my shoulders. "You must be Mark's bride. My name is Ruth." Her fingers felt cold on my arm, but her smile was warm and kind. "I attend worship services at the church," she explained. "I'm so happy for you both, and I'll be praying for you—that GOD will use you for His glory," she explained. "Let me show you some things you might need."

To my delight, we looked at some dresses and bonnets made of brightly colored cotton material. "You should have at least two dresses," she advised, "One to wear daily and one for special. You might want to get them a little big. You can always tie the sash to pull them in."

"Bigger?" I laughed softly. "You think I might spread out once I'm married?"

"Yes," she replied with a thoughtful nod. Ruth carefully sorted through a few dresses, which hung on a long pole along the back wall of the mercantile. "Once you're in the family way, you'll need more room in them," she replied, a matter of fact. What do you think of this one?" She pulled a blue calico dress from the rack and held it up in front of me. "This one was sewn by Sarah Miller. She lives just down the road from the pastor's house. She's an excellent seamstress. It should last you a good, long time if you like it. Let's get a look in the mirror, shall we?" She steered me to an old, full-length mirror that had scattered dark flecks of missing silver.

I held the frock up and carefully studied my reflection. The color was very becoming, but the dress was noticeably large, and it hung limply in front of me like an empty potato sack. Ruth stepped behind me, pulled the sash taught around my waist, and tied a bow. See how it snugs up?" She peeked over my shoulder to admire her handiwork. "I imagine it's going to get hot out there, too. Here in town, those fitted dresses are fine, but out there, a body's got to breathe," she explained. A moment later, she placed a simple ivory bonnet on my head. "Now, you look like a real pioneer woman." Ruth peered over my shoulder into the speckled mirror, and both of us stood quietly for a moment and reflected on the image.

"My late husband and I made our way here years ago when this area was still wilderness," Ruth finally said, wistfully. "I'd give anything to have him back. We could join you and Mark on Monday," she smiled. "He'd have liked that. He loved adventure, and I loved him. I'd have followed that man to the ends of the earth." She sighed and stood quietly, absorbed in her own thoughts. The bright chime of the bell, which hung above the mercantile door, brought her quickly back to the present.

"Let's take another look at that rack and pick you out another frock," she suggested. We chose a second dress, this one a cheerful green with tiny flowers; then she had me try on a pair of practical shoes. "Those fancy shoes of yours won't last a day out there on the trail. You'll be plumb miserable in them, and I imagine you'd get blisters."

Once Ruth was satisfied that she had me properly outfitted for the journey, she turned her attention toward Mark. "Looks like your handsome groom is busy picking out something special for you," she whispered softly, smiled, and nodded toward the mercantile store's counter. I turned to see what she was speaking of and saw Mark standing opposite the store's proprietor, intently examining the contents of a narrow wooden tray.

Ruth carefully folded the dresses and placed the bonnet on top. "Perhaps you should go see what he's up to," she coaxed. "I'll bring these up to the counter in just a moment.

Not wanting to intrude, I quietly sauntered to the counter and peeked over Mark's broad shoulder. He was intently examining a small assortment of rings – a few were ornate with precious gems; most were simple wedding bands. "I've been saving for this for a long time." He spoke so low that I wondered if he was speaking to me or himself. "What do you think?" He glanced briefly at me, then turned his attention back to the tray of assorted rings on the counter. "You'll be wearing them for a long time. You should have something that you like."

I eased up beside him and studied the tray of rings. "An engagement ring, too?"

He smiled. "We might be a small town, but we're not without some sophistication," he chided. "That's the latest trend, now, isn't it? A ring for engagement?"

I nodded. "But we're getting married in just two days."

"I can't have our children thinking that their father was cheap on their mother. Pick out the ones that you like."

I glanced sideways at Ruth, who stood quietly cradling the shoes and dresses in her arms. She beamed a broad smile back. My cheeks and neck grew hot. What would my choice of rings say about me to others along the way? Fancy or plain? What would a pastor's wife, a woman of God, choose? I said a silent prayer for wisdom, then settled on a small gold ring with a tiny diamond and a simple gold band – a choice which surprised, and perhaps pleased, my future husband.

"We'll take these." He handed them to the store clerk, who tried to hide his disappointment.

Ruth wrapped my new apparel in crisp, brown paper, and several men loaded our precious provisions into the back of the wagon. Mark tucked the rings into his front pocket, climbed back into the wagon, and reached both arms out to steady me as I stepped from the loading dock to the wagon seat. The brake groaned in complaint as he pulled the lever to release it, and the oxen's ears flicked back briefly in response to Mark's shrill whistle. They obediently leaned into their yoke, and our wagon eased forward, away from the mercantile store.

A few scattered clouds had chosen to lighten their load, and we found ourselves in a gentle sprinkle as the heavily laden wagon crept slowly back toward the pastor's home. "Spring rains!" Mark exclaimed happily. "We'll need those so that the grass on the prairie can feed our animals," he explained. "Otherwise, we would have to carry so much feed that it would be impossible for us to travel such a long distance."

Instead of turning toward home, we continued straight into town, where the team halted in front of the Hudson Hotel. "You might as well get your things while we are in

A Wagon, a Team of Oxen, and an Engagement Ring

town," Mark said, setting the brake. "Unless you think that you'll need me, I'll stay out here and watch our supplies." He climbed over me and then jumped down to the ground with a thud. I could feel his strong muscles flex as he steadied me and then gently planted my feet on the wooden sidewalk. Our bodies were so close that I flushed with embarrassment. With eyes cast sheepishly to the ground, I scurried away quickly to finish my business with the hotel.

Everything was exactly as I'd left it: tidy bed, dresses hung, and open windows. The room's white curtains, which alternately billowed then snapped, gave warning of an incoming storm. The window resisted any effort to close at first, but after several failed attempts at jiggling it back and forth, finally relented. I quickly gathered my few remaining possessions and, once tucked securely under one arm, trotted down the stairs. "I'm checking out," I informed the clerk, and with my hotel bill satisfied, quickly made my way out to an anxiously awaiting Mark.

Menacing dark clouds blanketed the sky above Marshall. I quickly tossed my dresses and boots into the back of the wagon and climbed onto the seat beside him. He whistled then clucked to our oxen, and we headed home as quickly as possible down the rutted dirt roads toward the Peterson's house.

Once the oxen team pulled the wagon into the yard, Mark quickly jumped down, grasped the nearest ox's nose ring, and led both the team and wagon into the Peterson's barn. Immediately, the heavens seemed to open, spilling thick, gray sheets of precious water. It promptly freshened and cooled the early spring air, and an exhilarated Mark let out a joyous shout, sending Pastor Peterson's mare prancing nervously in her stall. He quickly strode back to the wagon and gently lifted me to the ground beside him.

It was raining too hard to attempt a dash to the house, so we sat on prickly stacks of yellowish-brown hay and contentedly watched God water the land – a wedding gift that we needed so dearly!

The deluge of rain continued to rhythmically pound the barn roof in a soothing, hypnotic lullaby. My eyelids slowly grew heavy, so I wrapped my arms around my knees and rested my head on them. Mark yawned, then stretched backward onto the hay, but then quickly sat up with a start. I raised my head and turned to watch him. He reached into his pocket and then carefully lifted out the tiny engagement ring.

"I wish this could be more romantic, but we are about to be overwhelmed by a lot of people, and I'm not sure if we will get the chance to be alone again before the wedding."

My fingers trembled as he slipped the ring on; then, whether from true fondness or that we were now an engaged couple, he held my hand gently in his.

The back screened door of the Peterson's home flew open and smacked against the outside of the house with a resounding bang. A tall, slender figure, clad in rain slicker and hat, darted quickly out the door into the rain and headed straight toward the barn. Once inside, he let out a whoop, then tossed the hat onto a harness hook and quickly shook off the coat.

"Mama said I'd better come out and check on you two," he chided with a grin.

"Really?" Mark asked flatly. He didn't sound pleased that our moment had been interrupted.

"Naw." The man paused with a smile. "Too many women in the house. You know how they are when they start planning something."

Mark stood, and the two men embraced briefly. "Jonathan, this is my bride, Grace. Grace, this is my brother, Jonathan."

"Nice to meet you, Grace." He nodded politely, then turned back to his brother. "Have you two heard the latest plans that Mother has for you?" He grasped a yellow sprig of hay from a bale, then stuck one end in his mouth to chew.

"What plans are those?" Mark inquired cautiously.

"Well, tonight is family night, so everyone can have the chance to meet Grace. Tomorrow, they have a big barbecue and quilting. Saturday, we'll go down to the church for rehearsal. Sunday is the big day, and Mother and the girls are currently working on the reception details. She and the girls are planning to cook up a storm over the next few days. You know how Mother is about parties and celebrating," he chuckled. "So, this is the ark that is going to take you away?" He walked over to the oxen and gave the nearest one an affectionate pat on the back.

They forgot about me and were absorbed in the latest

family news while unharnessing the team. I sat on a hay bale, quietly listening and watching the rain as it slowly began to taper off into a gentle mist.

From their conversation, I surmised that everyone lived a good ride away, and they took special occasions to catch up on what the others were doing. Jonathan and his wife were expecting their third child in October. He was hoping that this one would be a boy. Their youngest sister, Hannah, was also expecting. This child would be the first of what they wished to be a large family. She and her husband had begun building their own home and hoped to finish it before the baby came. Their older sister, Rachel, was still childless after five years of marriage. She and her husband had decided that perhaps it was not God's will for them, and they were beginning to consider the possibility of adopting. Their mother had been assuring Rachel that there were many children without loving homes and that Jesus would be pleased if they did decide to open their home and hearts to a child in need of a family. She promised to help by asking around to see if anyone knew of a baby needing a loving home. Michael, the eldest, who had followed his father's footsteps into the ministry, had been offered a larger church; but it would take him and his family farther away than they wished.

Finally, Mark resumed his place beside me on the hay, and Jonathan pulled down the wagon's tailgate and sat on it. We sat in silence and enjoyed the fresh spring air that the rain had brought with it.

"Your time alone will end in approximately five minutes and probably won't resume for another six months," Jonathan surmised. He began chuckling at his own assessment of the situation. "I guess I'll be heading back to the house to give you two a few more moments of privacy." He stood, stretched, then pulled his hat off the hook and picked up the rain slicker. "Welcome to the family, Grace." He tipped the brim of his hat, then gave Mark a firm punch on his upper arm before sauntering back to the house.

Ten

Peterson Party Planners

An excellent wife who can find? She is far more precious than jewels.
Proverbs 31:10

    The heavy rainstorm left the yard dotted with large, dark pools. Mark had to steady me from slipping on patches of slick, pasty mud. I worried what an impression I might make to his sisters should I lose my footing. We cautiously wove our way across the yard until we reached the house without monumental incident.

    "Unka Mawk! Unka Mawk!" A small, angelic child with breathless blue eyes and a crown of soft, curly brown locks flew open-armed across the room toward us. "Peek me up!" she insisted. Mark obeyed and swung the child upward as she squealed with delight. A small parade of bright-eyed children suddenly appeared from adjoining rooms to surround their uncle. "Me too! Me too!" They chimed in unison – each hopping up and down with extended arms.

    Mark turned the little brown-haired girl to face me. "Sarah, this is going to be your Aunt Grace. Can you say hello to her?

    "Hewow," she said, with wide, curious eyes. "Awe you go'in to mawry Unka Mawk?"

    "Yes, I am." I managed an anxious smile, aware that

everyone within this close-knit family was examining me. *Lord, please let them like me.*

Mark gently lowered Sarah to the floor and picked up another child. This one was a bit taller, with longer curls – but quite obviously, a sibling of the first. "Grace, I would like you to meet Nita, Sara's older sister. They belong to Jonathan and Oneida."

"Hello, Nita," I smiled.

She smiled back at me shyly. "Uncle Mark, swing me!" she said, turning her attention quickly back to Mark. She giggled in anticipation.

He quickly swung her downward between his long legs and up above his head a few times before setting her gently down and picking up the next child.

This time he picked up a blonde boy about the same age as Nita, groaning as he did. "This big boy is Michael, Junior. He belongs to my oldest brother, Michael, and his wife, Lydia. "Michael, say hello to Grace."

"Hello, Miss Grace."

"Michael, you are getting heavy. Let's see if I can do this at all." He swung him only once, and gritting his teeth, he placed him quickly on the floor.

"All right, who's next?" he said, smiling down at the last two children, a boy, and a girl, and stretching backward to relieve his back.

"Me! Me!" they both shouted, jumping up and down in unison.

"Well, ladies first, Robert." He reached down for a

petite blonde girl with blue eyes. "Grace, this is Mary. She and Robert also belong to Michael and Lydia." He swung Mary a few times and then gave Robert his turn as well. "Whew!" He used the cuff of his sleeve to wipe the dampness from his face. "They're all getting so big!" he exclaimed.

"Too many books and not enough work!" A deep voice chided from the hallway behind us.

I turned to see a tall, muscular man leaning casually against the kitchen door. Soft gray streaks were just beginning to frost the temples of his sandy-brown hair. He had the same disarming blue eyes that the rest of the Peterson clan boasted. Clad in long, black trousers with suspenders and the same open-collared white shirt as Pastor Peterson, I gathered that this must be the eldest, Michael. He casually sauntered toward us and extended a warm hand to clasp mine.

"You must be Grace," he stated. "I know that you'll have so many names to remember, but I'm Michael. The last three children that Mark gave rides to were mine." He turned to Mark and smiled. "They're growing like weeds, aren't they?" His face beamed with pride.

"That they are," Mark agreed. "Especially Michael Junior! I hear that the ladies have quite a send-off planned for us. Do we need to run away, or are you willing to go ahead and marry us now in the parlor?"

They both laughed simultaneously, but I failed to see the humor of it. Was he joking, or was there a glimmer of his true feelings in what he said? I choked back my shyness and decided to speak up.

"Mark!" I exclaimed. "Whatever would we do that for?"

They laughed again, but this time Mark took the liberty of placing his arm around my waist and gave me a brief, discreet hug.

"Don't worry, Grace. Everything will go as planned. You may wish, though, that we did marry now." His arm dropped from my waist, and instead, he cupped his hand at the small of my back and gently steered me toward the parlor where wedding plans were in full bloom.

"Hold everything! Hold everything!" His booming voice announced our arrival. "You ladies would never dream of planning a wedding without the bride present, would you?"

The soft, feminine chatter in the room abruptly ceased, and all eyes turned to us. "Everyone, this is my bride-to-be, Grace. Grace, I would like to introduce the ladies of the family. You know my beautiful mother, Molly, whom I would certainly wed if she weren't already taken. Next to her, on the right, is Hannah, my youngest sister. She used to follow me everywhere when we were growing up. Next is Rachel, the most practical one of us all. Beside her is Lydia, Michael's lovely wife, and next is Oneida, who must have the patience of a Saint because she is married to Jonathan.

Hannah smiled, and the soft, welcoming expression on her face was kind. "Welcome to the family, Grace. Come join us, won't you?"

Of all Mark's siblings, Hannah looked most like their mother. Her long, dark blonde hair draped gently over her dainty shoulders and down her slender back. She wore a white dress with tiny blue flowers and small green leaves which swirled about. A modest, high collar around her neck framed the sweet, gentle expression on her young face. I hoped that we would get along splendidly.

"Yes, Grace, please join us." Mrs. Peterson gestured to the soft, leather, overstuffed chair next to her. A small fire crackled in the fireplace to chase away the cool dampness of today's rainstorm. "Of course, Mark, we would never dream of making plans without consulting Grace. But it was necessary to begin making some plans since your wedding day is only two days away. Don't you agree, Grace?"

Mark leaned forward and whispered softly into my ear, "Remember what I said about them and planning parties?"

I smiled at the Peterson ladies and settled into place next to Mark's mother. They all appeared cordial, but I was sure in my heart that they each had reservations about our plans. I chose not to take it personally, though. Why wouldn't they want the best for their brother? No doubt the wedding festivities were to please him, and they would know what things to plan.

"Of course, Mrs. Peterson. I certainly appreciate everything you are doing."

She smiled, very pleased with my response. Out of the corner of my eye, I could see a smile on Mark's face, too, as he quietly slipped out of the parlor.

"Grace, dear, I thought that tonight would be an ideal time for the family to spend some quality time together," Mrs. Peterson advised. I nodded attentively. "Tomorrow, the pastor and I have invited a few people over for a barbecue in your honor. It is a tradition around here for the ladies to get together to make a wedding quilt for the couple. I thought that since we only have a few days before you leave, the cook-out would be a perfect time to work on the quilt."

"That would be very nice," I agreed.

"The following day is Saturday and the last day before your wedding. We will need to make your wedding cake, and you and Mark will need to finish getting prepared." Her voice quivered briefly, but she quickly regained control. "Sunday will be the wedding, and you will leave early Monday morning."

This must be very difficult for her. My thoughts abandoned the small talk about wedding festivities, and I drifted in amazement at this strong woman of God. Could I fit into her shoes? A pastor's helpmate? I didn't think so – at least not yet, anyway, I surmised. She must have been a very brave young woman and, as a pastor's new wife, had moved very far away from everything that she held so dear. Now, her son was doing the same: taking the Gospel into an unknown future, away from all those who loved and cared for him. *Lord, let us be following Your plan.*

Lydia and Oneida quickly jumped up to investigate the sounds of uncontrolled childish chaos and laughter emanating from another room. The interruption brought the chat of the upcoming festivities to a close. Mrs. Peterson grasped the arms of her chair and pushed herself upward with a soft 'umph'.

"Girls, shall we go finish the evening meal? I'm sure everyone is starting to get hungry." Hannah and Rachel stood on cue, obeying their mother's lead. "Grace, I believe I have plenty of help. Why don't you take some time for yourself?" I nodded, glad for the opportunity to escape curious eyes.

Mrs. Peterson headed toward the kitchen to work on the evening's meal. Rachel and Hannah followed behind, but as they reached the hall, Hannah affectionately looped her arm through Rachel's and briefly laid her head on her sister's shoulder.

Taking advantage of my momentary reprieve from the evening's noise and excitement, I lingered in the parlor to allow them time to begin their work in the kitchen. My intent was to slip out the kitchen door and make my way to Mrs. Peterson's fragrant flower garden, but just as I reached the kitchen, I stopped short. I could hear that they were speaking of me.

"She's very pretty, so I can understand why Mark is drawn to her. What if, after a month on the trail, he finds out that she isn't a suitable wife? Pretty is as pretty does," Rachel commented.

"I think it all sounds wonderfully romantic!" Hannah exclaimed. "A new wife. Adventure. Beautiful country.

Interesting people. It sounds amazing to me." Next, Hannah's husband chimed in.

"You want'n to go, too, on Monday?" he chided. "Abandon the house and move into a wagon? Have our first child alongside the trail?"

I could hear Hannah's gentle laugh at her husband's question.

"Girls." Mrs. Peterson cut the conversation short. "Your father inquired into her character. She seems to be just as she appears: a nice young woman. Besides, even if she changed her mind, I believe that Mark would set out on Monday without her. He has everything that he needs to go, and he's excited about it. It's better that she goes with him. They'll have plenty of time to get to know each other before they reach their destination.

It pinged my heart that I caught them speaking of me. I had come to love this family and wanted them to approve of me. Too embarrassed to walk in following their conversation, I turned on my heel and made my way out the front door, around the corner of the house, and out to Mrs. Peterson's garden.

The middle of the garden boasted a lovely, ornate white metal bench, and once I planted myself there, I enjoyed the gentle hum of busy bees going about their daily chores. I was deep in thought when Mark quietly joined me on the bench. After a bit of silence, he whispered," Are you having any second thoughts?"

"No. Not really," I replied.

"Me either."

We sat quietly enjoying each other's company and watched an amazing sunset displaying God's glory until a shout from the house called us into the evening meal.

Eleven
The Quilting

And we know that for those who love God all things work together for good, for those who are called according to his purpose. Romans 8:28

Friday morning, people began to arrive in droves, and there was activity everywhere in and around the house. Lydia and Oneida were busy preparing the children for company while Hannah and Rachel helped Mrs. Peterson in the kitchen. My job, as Mrs. Peterson instructed, was to make myself as presentable as a blushing bride should and to practice my finest manners throughout the day.

I had decided to wear my new, mint-green calico dress which fit me well and heightened the color in my cheeks. Mrs. Peterson lent me a pair of her soft, kid-skin shoes, which were so comfortable that it felt as if I were walking on air. Whether I looked it or not, I felt very pretty in my new clothes and, in a light-hearted mood, began to hum a tune softly to myself while I brushed my hair. A gentle rap at the door caught my attention, and as I opened it, Oneida was standing at the door, her hair not yet addressed, holding a very sour-faced Sara.

"Grace, I hate to bother you since this is supposed to be your very special day, but could you watch Sarah for me? I'm afraid that she woke up quite a handful this morning, and I can't seem to get myself ready." Her eyes were damp and slightly reddened, and I could hear frustration in her voice.

"Yes, of course," I said. "I'm afraid that I haven't much experience with children, though."

Oneida looked relieved. "Oh, thank you, Grace!" she exclaimed. "You don't really have to do anything with her – just keep her out of trouble until I'm presentable!"

With that, she deposited little Sarah quickly on my bed and disappeared out the door. The child who had appeared so angelic yesterday resembled a tiny demon this morning. Her curly brown hair was tousled, and her little face was puckered into a defiant scowl. She had her arms crossed tightly, and her dark blue eyes glared piercing daggers at me.

With a deep breath of resolve, I attempted to initiate peace between myself and the tiny Beelzebub on my bed. "Good morning, Sarah!" Would you like me to brush your hair?" I leaned toward her with my brush. A terrible, loud shrieking noise came out of her mouth. "Hush, Sarah! Hush!" I whispered, then quickly closed the bedroom door. She finally ceased but continued her glare.

Thinking it best to leave well enough alone, I turned to the mirror and began brushing my hair. The creaking of the door caught my attention, and as I turned back around to face the bed, a surprise awaited me. The child was gone!

The Quilting

I dropped the hairbrush and darted out of the door. There was no Sarah to be seen in the hallway. How could someone so small move so quickly?

I made a quick check of the rooms, tapping gently on each door before I opened them. No, Sarah. My heart sank with the realization that I now had to tell her mother. As I tapped on the last door, Oneida's soft voice answered me.

"Yes?"

How did you tell someone that you had lost their child? When she opened her door, she looked a little confused. "Oneida, I don't know how to tell you . . . but I have lost Sarah." The worried look on her face said it all. I had done a terrible thing, turning my back on such a small child. "Oh, Oneida, I'm so sorry! I turned my back for just a second, and she was gone!"

Oneida was out of the room and flew down the stairs before I could finish. "We'll have to find her quickly before she gets hurt or into trouble!" she shouted back to me.

"Oh, Lord! Please don't let Sarah get lost or hurt!" I frantically whispered. "Please keep her safe wherever she is and let me find her!"

Once in the kitchen, Oneida caught Rachel by the arm, and they began a search downstairs. I quickly ran out the back door. Frightened tears began to stream out of the edges of my eyes. I ran toward the barn quickly scanning the groups of visitors who had arrived for the day's festivities.

"Sarah! Sarah? Are you in here?" I shouted as I entered the dimly lit barn. A tiny voice called out from one of the stalls.

"Ant Gwace? Come see wat I fond."

I held my breath as I made my way down the hay-strewn aisle.

"See wat I have, Ant Gwace?"

Sarah stood in the stall, firmly grasping the nose ring of one of our new oxen. My heart dropped at the sight. He was massive next to this tiny child.

"Sarah, honey, let go of the ox and come here," I instructed softly.

"Ant Gwace, can I keep him? I theek I cawl heem Buddercup." She patted his dark, wet nose with her tiny hand. The ox stood still with his eyes closed.

"Sarah, honey, stay real still next to Buttercup, all right?" I made my way cautiously toward the tiny tot and the massive ox and slowly lifted the child into my arms. "Sarah, you mustn't do that again!" I fussed. We walked out of the stall, and I latched the door securely behind us. Buttercup stood quietly chewing his cud.

"Thank You, Lord, that You gave Mark the wisdom to buy us oxen instead of mules! And thank You for letting me find Sarah safe and sound." With the precious package safely in my arms, I quickly left the barn in search of her mother.

The Quilting

"Sarah, you mustn't run off like that ever again!" Oneida instructed her child with a stern voice. "You could have gotten hurt very badly." She lifted a messy Sarah into her trembling arms, then walked up the stairs to freshen them both. At the top of the stairs, she stopped and turned back to me. "Thank you, Grace, for finding her. I'm afraid that this was a terrible beginning to your happy day." She turned and walked away, disappearing down the upstairs hallway.

Mrs. Peterson gently grasped my arm and pulled me out the front door with her. She looked stunning in a blue cotton dress with a high collar, a ruffle around the waist, and small, puffed sleeves. Her hair was twisted fashionably on top of her head and secured with several matching blue hairpins. "Where on Earth have you been, Grace? I've been looking for you," She advised.

The morning sun had already risen well up into the cloudless blue spring sky. A soft, gentle breeze ruffled the tender green leaves that had recently sprouted from the Maple tree in their front yard. Various sizes and types of wagons were parked alongside the road. Several teams of horses and mules grazed contentedly on the thick green grass next to them, stretching their tethers as far as possible. Their tails lazily swished back and forth, repelling flies that buzzed around them.

"There are so many people who you must meet." Mark's mother firmly guided me around the corner of the house toward a group of ladies. "Grace," she continued, "These ladies are going to sew you a wedding ring quilt today. It will be something that you can remember this day by for many years." She briefly introduced each quilter to me – there were twelve of them in all. Although I received friendly smiles from each of them, I surmised that they were curious about Mark's sudden engagement but perhaps too polite to ask.

"Thank you very much." I hoped that my voice sounded sincere rather than nervous. "I know that we will look at this quilt fondly and remember each of you for many years."

Mrs. Peterson smiled, pleased with my response. It made me glad that I had paid attention at Miss Tilden's Ladies Finishing School. Many of the girls giggled, whispered, and paid little attention to Miss Tilden when she spoke. I had always envisioned that after school, I would marry a notable man, travel, meet very important people, and wear fine gowns and jewelry. Today, my groom was truly a notable man, having chosen to serve and follow Christ. I had no doubt that we would be meeting many people from all walks of life. My wedding gown was borrowed, our travel would be westward, and my jewelry was a thin gold band with a tiny diamond chip. My heart was full of joy, and I was truly happy.

A willowy young woman with long brown hair joined the group, carrying a parcel wrapped in brown paper. "I

The Quilting

have the backing!" she said cheerfully. She smiled warmly at me and extended her hand, briefly clasping mine in a friendly gesture. "Hello, you must be Grace. My name is Eunice," she said with a generous, toothy smile. "I was the last bride to get a quilt, so it was my turn to bring the backing this time." She extended her left hand out to proudly display the thin gold band around her finger.

"Nice to meet you," I responded with a smile. "Thank you for coming today and for bringing the quilt backing."

Mark, his brothers, and a few other young men carried a large table and sat it down next to where the group of quilters had assembled. Another gentleman brought a large quilting frame and sat it next to the table, and still, several others carried various styles of kitchen chairs and set them around the table.

"You ladies need anything else?" Mark asked. His question was met with several replies from the group.

"No. That's it. Thank you, Mark!"

"Thank you, gentlemen!"

"I believe that's all we need right now. Thank you!"

Each woman placed her own brightly colored quilting bag on the table, and while colorful scraps of material began to appear from them, happy, light-hearted conversation began. The ladies had already created colorful circles from their scrap material, and they quickly filled the tabletop with a rainbow of calico.

"Grace, what colors would you like us to use?" Mrs. Peterson asked. All eyes turned to me.

"Oh!" I exclaimed, both pleased and surprised that they would create it to my liking. "I'm partial to blues and greens," I confessed, "but they are all lovely."

A young, attractive woman with raven-colored hair and green eyes held up a circle that had been made from the same material as the green frock I wore. "Grace! Look at this!" she laughed.

"I definitely want that one!" I laughed with her and swished the skirt of my dress so that the others would understand as well.

"Blue and green it is, then, so let's get started!" Mrs. Peterson exclaimed.

Suddenly, the quilting party was off to a marvelous start with a flurry of conversation, laughter, and activity. A white sheet of material was stretched on the quilting frame, and the ladies began to expertly position green and blue calico fabric circles on it, carefully pinning each one into place. Having successfully accomplished the task to their satisfaction, they each placed a chair at the quilting frame and, with thread and needle in hand, began to skillfully stitch the circles onto the top of the quilt.

The Quilting

A plump, white-haired woman in a light brown dress patted the empty chair next to her. "Grace, why don't you sit next to me?" She reached into the large canvas bag by her chair and brought out another sewing needle, then expertly maneuvered thick white thread through the needle's eye and quickly tied a knot in it.

"I'm Annie Mae," she said as she passed the threaded needle to me. Her hands shook a bit as she did. "I'm probably the oldest one here. That don't bother me none, though. It's what's inside a person that matters. As a matter of fact, I attended the birth of many of the young ladies who are here quilting." She paused, then realized that I was intently watching the skillful handiwork of the other quilters. "You can start here, honey. Take a few minutes and watch how the other ladies make their stitches before you begin. Take your time and do it well. It should last for a lifetime if you do. Be careful that you don't prick yourself. If you get blood on these quilts, it is almost impossible to get it out."

Following her advice, I sat for several minutes, just watching the other ladies making tiny, expert stitches with experienced hands. With a deep sigh of resolution, I carefully plunged my needle into the edge of a bright blue calico ring and made a crooked stitch.

Annie Mae's chair creaked softly as she leaned over to look. "That's all right, honey. What is one stitch in such a large quilt? Years from now, you will look for that crooked stitch to show your own daughters how you did at first. Don't get discouraged! Keep going."

I bit my lip sharply and leaned forward to make another stitch. This time I managed to get it somewhat straighter. The next stitch was nearly perfect. Encouraged by my success, I continued to judiciously follow the curve of the ring.

"Every piece of material on your quilt came from pieces of the lives of each of these ladies. It represents the love they have for their families. See that young woman with red hair?" Annie Mae continued, "You'll notice that she likes to use a lot of green-colored material. That's Agatha Miller. That dark green calico she's sewing on your quilt is from one of her favorite dresses she used to wear. She wore it when she was being courted by her husband. The material next to it, with the tiny blue and green flowers, was one of the first outfits she made for their little baby. The green and white checkered ring came from a shirt she made her husband. It was the first thing she sewed for him, and it was purely awful. 'Course, I never actually saw him in it, but I heard-tell that when he tried it on, they both laughed and placed the thing in the scrap bag together. People think that I'm old, but I sure can remember things real good – sometimes better than they can!" she laughed.

Annie Mae was delightful. She continued to clue me in 'on the goods', as she put it, about everyone who was attending our quilting. By the time she finished with me, I

The Quilting

could recite who was married to whom, how many children they had, what color material each woman preferred to purchase, and whether they attended church regularly. She caused me to laugh more than just a few times.

Little Sarah, who had been so much trouble this morning, managed to wiggle up onto my lap. She wanted to watch the quilting from a very strategic position. The difficulty that I had making suitable stitches was heightened by her incessant wiggling.

"Sarah, honey," I whispered softly into her little ear, "Wouldn't you rather be with the other children playing or with your mama?"

"No," she said, defiantly shaking her brown curly locks. "I want to be wif you!" The latter she accented as if it should be a great honor. There seemed no sense in trying to reason with her lest she cause a scene and embarrass the Peterson family.

An anxious tug at my shoulder made me turn, and I was surprised to see Rachel, Mark's sister, standing behind me.

"Grace," she spoke softly, "may I speak to you for a moment?"

"Of course," I replied. I pinned my needle securely to the quilt, lifted Sarah off my lap, and placed her in the chair. "Would you see to it that this prisoner doesn't escape?" I asked Annie Mae. "She has already given us quite a start this morning."

"I sure will, honey," she replied with a good-natured chuckle, then turned to Sarah. "Honey, why don't you sit on Annie Mae's lap? I'll just bet my lap is the softest one you've ever sat on."

Sarah nodded and was immediately scooped up by Annie's ample arms and placed securely onto her lap. Satisfied that Sarah was occupied for the moment, I followed Rachel around the corner of the house to see what she needed.

"Oh, Grace!" Rachel began, "One of the families here said that there is an elderly woman right outside of town whose only son and his wife were killed a few weeks ago. They were traveling across a bridge when it collapsed under them. Unfortunately, they drowned, leaving his mother to care for their two small children. She's in poor health and is unable to care for them. They said that they'd heard she would be willing to let a fine couple have them for their own if they'd let her see them, just as if she were still their grandmother. "Oh, Grace!" she said, beginning to bounce slightly in excitement, "There is a little girl two years old and a three-month-old boy. Would you mind terribly if Thomas and I slipped away from your party for a little while to go see about the children?"

Of course, I knew that Rachel was only asking to be polite. Wild horses could not have kept her away from those children. "Yes, of course, Rachel!" I gave her a reassuring hug. "You must go and see about the children."

The Quilting

She briefly hugged me back and ran to join a small wagon with another young couple and her husband, Thomas. Thomas reached down and grasped her arms, lifting her easily into the wagon next to him. They hugged briefly, and with a face full of excitement, Rachel turned and waved at me before the wagon hastily retreated down the dirt road. It seemed a good idea to pray about this important matter; so, lifting my skirts to avoid the few remaining puddles from yesterday's rain, I went in search of Mark.

I found him painting beef with sauce at the barbecue pit while Pastor Peterson and a few other men were teasing him about married life. Even Mark was smiling. It was all in good fun.

"Mark, could I have a few moments with you?" I smiled and clasped my hands anxiously behind my back while rocking to and fro on my heels.

"Yes, certainly," he replied and handed the gooey barbecue rag to his father. "Is everything all right?" We strolled slowly away from the group that surrounded the pit.

"Yes, of course," I responded quickly. "Everyone has been so friendly! But something has come up which I thought I should share with you," I continued. "Rachel and Thomas have gone to see about two young orphan children just outside of town."

His eyebrows arched upward in surprise, and he looked at me with great interest. "Does anyone else know about this?" He lowered his voice to a near whisper.

I whispered as well. "Perhaps your mother?" I guessed. "Rachel wanted to be sure about the children first."

"We could pray for them," Mark suggested. "I'd hate for Rachel to be disappointed. She's waited and prayed so long for children."

We slipped into the cool, quietness of the barn, away from our party visitors. The sound of contented munching of hay filled the air. Mark directed us toward our wagon, where he lifted me up onto the lowered tailgate, then hopped effortlessly on beside me. I felt the strong but gentle grasp of his hand on mine, and it made my heart leap.

"Lord Jesus," he began, "You know how badly Rachel and Thomas have wanted children, and only You know why You have caused them to wait. Perhaps it's because you knew that these children would need a loving home and that Rachel and Thomas could provide one. Please help them, Lord. Please let everything go well as they see about these children. Amen."

It was a short prayer – void of any elegant language or phrases, but we were satisfied that what needed to be done had been accomplished.

Twelve

Children For Rachel

For this child I prayed; and the LORD hath given me my petition which I asked of him: 1Samuel 1:27

The barbeque beef was delicious, and everyone appeared to eat their fill. Most of the ladies, including myself, found it difficult to keep the sauce from smudging around our mouths and dropping on our clothing as we ate – forcing us to take small, dainty bites. The children, of course, bothered little with attempting to keep clean, and were obviously going to be quite a challenge to scrub after the meal.

Little Sarah sat next to her mother, contentedly gnawing on a large meaty rib. She had reddish-brown sauce smeared around her face and even had streaks of it in her brown, curly hair. How could one child get so dirty; and how could barbeque sauce end up in one's hair? My questions were answered when Sarah lifted one small, gooey hand to scratch her curly head. A new layer of reddish sauce compounded her already messy brown locks, making them droop heavily down. Her mother, Oneida, continued to quietly eat her meal beside Sarah, paying little attention to the disaster happening right within her reach.

I looked at my own fingers. They were just as messy as Sarah's, although I had tried diligently to keep them clean. Now, they were sticky with the reddish-brown sauce, too, and there was not a napkin in sight.

Occasionally, a curious comment was made inquiring about the absence of Rachel and Thomas. Pastor and Mrs. Peterson began to voice concerns themselves until Mark took them inside the house to discuss the matter privately. Eventually, the three of them joined the party again with excited smiles of relief. Mrs. Peterson's cheeks were unusually rosy, and her earlier anxiety caused by the upcoming wedding appeared to have been swept away.

With a deep sigh of accomplishment, Mark reclaimed his seat on the long wooden bench next to me and settled back down to his half-finished plate of ribs. He bit down on the pit-darkened meat, chewing slowly to savor the taste, then glanced sideways at me with a light-hearted grin. "It's so good," he admitted, then watched with amusement as I carefully nibbled on my own meal. "You need to eat well now, Grace. We won't eat as well out on the trail, come Monday."

I returned his smile, and when I did, I caused the rib to bump up against my cheeks, branding my face with a respectable glob of sauce. Yes, I thought there would be very few meals in the future as good as this, so he'd better enjoy it.

Children For Rachel

The return of Rachel and Thomas caused quite a stir. The wooden wagon rattled noisily into the yard, summoning a large group of curious friends. Both sat quietly in the back of the wagon, beaming with pride. Thomas gently cuddled a small girl with curly blonde hair and stunning gray eyes. She looked awestruck by the unusual events of the day and, as the group of onlookers approached the wagon, began to cry and hold tightly to her new father.

Rachel held a small bundle in her arms, wrapped snugly in a colorful cradle quilt. As Pastor and Mrs. Peterson wound their way carefully through the crowd, she unwrapped the little boy's tiny head. He was deep asleep, but his soft gray eyelashes fluttered like butterflies as he dreamt, and his tiny rosebud mouth made smacking noises on a tightly clenched fist.

"Mama. Papa. This is your little grandson Gabriel, and your granddaughter, Emily," Rachel announced with a wide, beaming smile.

Mrs. Peterson covered her mouth and gasped. A gentle flood of tears began to stream down her face. "Thank You, Jesus," she whispered.

There were now two joyous events to be celebrated by the Peterson's. Everyone exclaimed their best wishes to the new family. Pastor and Mrs. Peterson helped them down from the wagon and into the house with their new children. It was obvious that Emily had enough excitement for the day, and the quickly approaching evening, with its mosquitoes and gnats, was no place for a tiny baby as well.

Mark and his brothers unloaded a cradle along with a few of the children's clothes and carried them into the house. For part of the Peterson family, the party was over. Hannah, gracious but quiet, resumed her mother's duties as hostess. She strolled about the crowd, politely exchanging small talk and seeing to their needs. A few of the guests with small children excused themselves, taking their own young families home to be washed and tucked into bed. An elderly gentleman with thick gray hair and a long, stringy beard brought out a fiddle and began to entertain the group with lively toe-tapping music.

Everyone quickly gathered around him, clapping happily to the tune. Mark suddenly grabbed both my hands and began to twirl me around. His feet stepped lightly to the sweet music, and although the steps were unfamiliar to me, I found that he was easy to follow.

Someone within the group gave a festive yelp, and several young couples joined in with us. We danced non-stop, whirling around the large circle with carefully calculated steps. Exhausted and out of breath, I finally had to beg Mark for a short rest. With a regretful smile, he left me sitting back on the wooden bench but easily replaced me with Annie Mae – whirling her lightly away into the crowd, much to her delight.

Children For Rachel

For a while, I watched the happy crowd prance joyously to the delightful music of the fiddle and clapped my hands along. But once I sat still, I could tell just how long the day had been. My arms and legs ached terribly, and my fingers felt stiff from quilting. I looked over at the completed quilt, which hung on display across a white cotton cord strung between two maple trees in the Peterson's yard. The colors had become almost indistinguishable in the grayish light, but I knew in my heart that it held small pieces of each woman's life, sewn lovingly into intertwining circles.

I slipped quietly into the house unnoticed by the well-wishers. The main activity appeared to be in the kitchen, where Lydia and Oneida were busy trying to scrub the remnants of a good party, barbecue sauce, and dirt from the bodies of their children. Sarah, of course, was screaming in protest that she didn't need a bath and was not tired as her mother struggled to remove her filthy dress. Michael Junior sat quietly at the kitchen table reading a book by the soft light of the kerosene lamp. His damp hair was neatly combed into place, and a plain white cotton nightshirt replaced the party clothes that he'd worn earlier. Nita, Jonathan and Oneida's oldest daughter, sat beside him playing with a doll. Her long, curly brown hair had been washed and was now tamed into a simple braid. The soft light of the kerosene lamp gave her face an angelic glow. Robert and Mary, Michael and Lydia's younger children sat patiently on the floor, awaiting their turn. Their clothes boasted a day of hard play in the dirt and a delicious dinner with plenty of sauce. Thomas and Mrs. Peterson had retreated to the quietness of an upstairs bedroom to help little Emily prepare for bed. Anxious to find a quiet place to settle, I walked down the hallway toward the parlor.

There was a cozy fire in the fireplace, warming the damp night air in the Peterson's parlor. Rachel and little Gabriel were snuggled together in a wooden rocking chair. Soft, reassuring creaking came from the rocker as Rachel lulled Gabriel to sleep, back and forth. I smiled at her motherly blissfulness and turned to allow them this time alone.

"Grace, please come back," Rachel whispered before I could get far. "Do sit down and stay awhile," she said softly. Gabriel stirred, and she snuggled him a bit closer. He gave a tiny sigh of contentment and smiled sweetly in his sleep.

I sat on the edge of the parlor's sofa. Perhaps one day, I would be in her place, rocking and cuddling my own new baby.

"I just wanted to thank you for coming here to us," she smiled. "I believe that you came here for a reason, Grace. If you had not come, you would not be engaged to Mark, Mama, and Papa wouldn't have had the party, and Thomas and I wouldn't have met the couple who knew about the children. I believe that I am holding my new son and Thomas and Mama with little Emily because you came." She continued, "If it was God who brought you here, your obedience to Him has already been a great blessing to our family." She paused to gaze at the tiny new life in her arms. "The Bible says that we are predestined as to whether we will become children of God or not. That means that God already knows which trail we will choose to follow. Perhaps as you stepped out to follow His trail, He led you here to follow a special trail that you were destined to follow."

Tiny Gabriel began to squirm again, and Rachel resumed her gentle rocking to comfort her new son. Having been given something to think about, I quietly slipped from the room to allow them time alone together.

By the time I slipped out into the yard, the guests had begun to tire and only a few continued to dance. The elderly, gray-haired fiddler looked exhausted, and his arms, once upward, sagged with the weight of the instrument.

Hannah was busy clearing soiled dishes from the tables and gathering bones that had fallen to the ground. Like me, she had no children yet with which to excuse herself from the chores. And with the excitement of Gabriel and Emily, the task of cleaning up had been forgotten by the other women in the family. I spied a half-eaten rib and retrieved it, stretching the kinks from my aching back as I slowly stood.

"This time next year, you'll be inside with the others," I gestured toward her small, round tummy.

"Yes," she replied happily. "And if you and Mark go, who will be left to clean the mess?"

I smiled and laughed softly in agreement. Within such a short time, I'd become very fond of this family; and the thought of leaving them so soon made me a bit melancholy. Mark was so excited about the trip west it would be impossible to talk him out of going now. Besides, if we decided not to go, did that mean that the wedding plans were off? I picked up a gooey plate from the table and looked at the barbecue pit where the men of the family had gathered. Were Michael and the pastor giving Mark advice regarding married life?

The few young women who remained joined in to help Hannah and me with the dishes. We carried the soiled plates to the well's pump, where a barrel had been sawn in two to serve as a sink. Hannah washed, and one of the ladies worked the pump to rinse; two other ladies and I dried and placed the dishes in neat stacks on a wooden table. With many hands pitching in, the task was accomplished quickly.

Mark wandered away from the barbecue pit to join me so that we could thank the few remaining couples for coming. He affectionately looped his arm through mine, and we sauntered slowly around the house where mule and horse teams were busy being harnessed and hitched back to their wagons. His parents joined us to wave a last farewell to their guests as the line of wagons began their slow journey down the dirt road for home.

With the guests gone, it was suddenly silent, and we were quickly plunged into darkness as the final bit of the sun's rays moved below the horizon. The song of crickets began to fill the air, and somewhere in the distance, a solitary owl hooted, "Hu-hooooo! Hu-hooooo!"

The pastor sighed deeply with exhaustion and, with a firm hand wrapped affectionately around his wife's waist, slowly steered her back through the front door. Finally, alone, Mark and I strolled leisurely toward where our new quilt hung and took it down before the evening's dew could dampen it.

"Wasn't that wonderful about little Emily and Gabriel? I'm so happy for Rachel and Thomas," I commented. Mark nodded quietly in agreement and stifled a weary yawn. The men of the family had been up very early to prepare the meat for the party.

He opened the back door, and we stepped into an empty kitchen. The faint sound of snoring could be heard drifting from upstairs. We parted company at the stairway without the passionate fanfare that another engaged couple might sneak if they were left alone at such a tempting hour. Mark, weary from the festivities and the early day, gave me a short peck on the cheek and sauntered slowly up the stairs to his room. I sighed deeply and waited until I heard his door click closed, then climbed the stairs myself. A hot bath would have felt good, but I settled instead for a light washing in the bowl on my washstand. Too tired to care, I discarded the idea of brushing my hair and crawled wearily onto the bed fully clothed. Exhaustion caused me to sleep as one who had joined the dead, except for a few moments during the early morning hours when I could hear the faint cries of a tiny baby.

Thirteen

Sisters to the Rescue

Therefore, as God's chosen people, holy and dearly loved, clothe yourselves with compassion, kindness, humility, gentleness and patience. Colossians 3:12

The household had been deep in activity well before I finally decided to crawl out of bed. Either because everyone wished to pamper me or that I would have been in the way, no one knocked on my door. For a moment, I attempted to bury my head under a soft, feather pillow to block out the loud clamor of children as they ate breakfast and then their boisterous shouts of warfare as they quickly rushed out to play.

It was supposed to be a busy day today, and I knew that I could not remain in bed; however, when I attempted to get up, my body was racked with pain. I'd surely overdone myself yesterday and would be forced to pay for it today.

Easing my bare feet to the floor, I slid one foot in front of the other until I made my way to the mirror above the washstand. Wild pieces of blonde hair stood out here and there, and my eyes had thin red streaks running through them as if I'd been awake all night. What a beautiful bride I would make! Surely in this condition, I would shuffle down the aisle as if I were an elderly woman. A soft tapping at the door summoned me.

"Yes?" I asked. Even my voice sounded painful. Hannah's sweet voice drifted musically toward me through the bedroom's wooden door.

"Grace?" Are you all right in there?" she inquired softly. "Everyone else has been up for hours. Are you well?"

I cracked the door slightly to allow her to slip in discreetly. "It's my body," I whined softly. "I can't move."

Hannah looked at me and frowned in sympathy. "Oh my!" She paused with her head cocked sideways and both hands on her hips. "This will not do at all today, Grace. We must get you going!" She pursed her lips together and began to think quickly how best to undo my present circumstance. "You stay right here. I'm going to heat some water." She quickly turned and disappeared out the bedroom door. I could hear the solid clanking of heavy metal on the stove as she set about her task.

Soon, I could hear the soft voices of the Peterson women deep in conversation, although I couldn't tell what was being said. Shortly, Oneida appeared in the room carrying a very large metal washtub. She quickly scooted my bed against the wall and placed the tub in the center of the room before disappearing out the door. Shortly, she reappeared with an ugly brown bottle which she placed on the washstand.

Rachel joined the rescue group by carrying pot after pot of steaming hot water, which was poured into the metal tub. After it had been sufficiently filled, she slowly emptied the contents of the brown bottle into the tub. The room was immediately filled with the pungent odor of horse liniment!

"I can't bathe in that!" I protested.

"Either bathe in that or shuffle around today like an elderly woman. Worse yet, what if you're still just as stiff tomorrow?" Oneida reasoned.

My future sisters-in-law gathered in the room with their arms crossed, awaiting my decision. They were right. I could barely move from the room, much less down the church aisle. Tossing aside all modesty, I dropped the wrinkled, green calico dress to the floor and allowed them to assist my aching body into the steaming pool of horse liniment.

Oneida and Rachel slipped quietly from the room, but Hannah knelt carefully beside the tub and began to untangle my wildly arrayed hair with a soft brush.

"Ow!" I moaned pitifully. First, my body, now my head.

"Grace, stop whining like a baby," Hannah insisted. She began working on a large knot in my hair. "I understand that some of the homesteaders moving west must walk the entire way. What if you end up walking? All I can say is that you better be prepared for some hardships."

After many tugs and pulls, she finally managed to tame my unruly hair, then plaited it in a simple, neat braid. "You'd better spend some time soaking – but Mark said that you're supposed to attend a meeting later today with the wagon train, so don't stay too long." With her final instruction, she left me to soak leisurely in the tub. The water was still steaming, and except for the foul smell of the horse liniment, it was just what my aching body needed.

Less than an hour later, I emerged from the guest room well-clothed in my blue calico dress and my hair neatly braided from Hannah's handiwork. Although I was still a bit sore and stiff, I was able to walk without the pitiful shuffling gait I'd suffered earlier.

The house was quiet except for the familiar creaking of the rocker in the parlor. *Rachel and Gabriel*, I surmised. Not wishing to disturb them, I slipped quietly out the kitchen door and into Mrs. Peterson's sunny garden.

The garden was quiet except for two small sparrows that chirped to each other as they hopped along the neatly furrowed rows in search of an afternoon meal. Mittens the kitten was also there, curled under a faded wooden bench. Her dainty white paws twitched spastically as she slumbered in its shade. Years of rain and sun had bleached the bench to a light gray and raised the bench's wooden grain making it rough and uneven. Among the garden company was also a tiny ladybug resting on the soft green leaf of a tomato plant. She fluttered her reddish-orange wings and waited quietly on the leaf for dinner to arrive. From this location, I could hear the faint laughter of children and an occasional word spoken by an adult drifting outward from the barn area. I meandered slowly through the fragrant garden for a bit, then headed toward the barn to search for Mark and his family.

The men were all busy painting something on our wagon's canvas top. Oneida, Hannah, Lydia, and Mrs. Peterson stood back to watch while ensuring that the children were well out of the way. Little Emily had obviously adjusted well to her new surroundings. She was busy toddling after the other children, tightly holding a tiny bouquet of spring flowers in her little hand. The older children were engaged in a game of follow-the-leader. Of course, Michael Junior, being the eldest, was leading. He had his small group of followers mimicking very silly actions as they marched energetically around the area where the men worked. I joined the ladies to watch the work being performed on the wagon's canvas top.

"They're putting linseed oil on the canvas," Mrs. Peterson explained. "It should help keep you and your things dry," she continued.

Mark caught sight of me and flashed an excited grin before going back to the task at hand. For a moment, I wondered if I'd get weary of the long trip and regret that we had even started. Although it was not cold, I shivered and then crossed my arms to warm the tiny bumps that had appeared on them. Dear sweet Hannah noticed and moved closer to me. She slipped a dainty arm around my shoulder to cuddle me as only a beloved sister would.

Once the canvas was painted to the men's satisfaction, Mark checked his pocket watch for the time. "Grace, we'll be needing to head toward the wagons for a meeting. I'll go hitch the buggy. You ready to go?"

I smiled at my young, handsome groom and gave my sweet sister-in-law, Hannah, a big hug. Mark's enthusiasm was infectious, and Hannah's comfort was reassuring. With renewed confidence, I followed Mark to watch him harness and hitch the pastor's mare, hoping that I might learn something from it.

The midmorning spring air felt refreshing as a gentle breeze flowed softly over my tired body. If Mark was feeling any effects from yesterday, he didn't show it. He snapped a lead to the mare's halter, swung open her stall door, and quickly led her to the Peterson's smart-looking black buggy. She stood quietly while Mark retrieved her harness and bridle, slipped it easily on, and we were soon ready to depart.

Because of yesterday's party, I was able to recognize some of the Peterson's neighbors as we rolled along the dusty dirt road. Eunice, one of the young women from the quilting, was out in her yard hanging her freshly washed laundry on a white chord stretched between two trees. There was a small brown dog with long hair sitting rigidly beside her laundry basket, faithfully guarding it. She saw me and waved as we passed her home.

"Hello! Mark, Grace! Beautiful day, isn't it?"

I smiled and waved back. "Hello, Eunice. Yes, it is!"

We passed by Annie Mae's house, too. She was sitting on her wide-columned porch, enjoying the pleasant spring morning. Her ample body rocked back and forth in a large rocking chair which creaked in protest. "Good morning, Annie!" I turned sideways in the buggy so that I could continue to see her as we drove past.

"Good morning, Grace." She shouted to reach my ears as we passed by. "Where ya'll heading to?" I felt confident that the information would be dispersed to the rest of the neighbors.

"Wagon train meeting!" Mark shouted back. She nodded her head. "No sense making her agonize about it," he advised. "Might as well give her something to talk about when someone else passes by." He grinned boyishly. "Bye, Annie!" he shouted. We rolled beyond the shouting distance of her home, so I turned back to my seat and sat properly.

Mark clucked to the mare and gently slapped the reins across her backside. The beautiful spring morning was intoxicating even to her, and if Mark had allowed it, she might have pulled over to nap under a tree. He made her pick up the pace to an easy jog.

With the soft breeze blowing on my face, I dreamily closed my eyes and allowed my mind to wander. I had promised Claudia that I would keep in touch to let her know what had happened to me. This would be the first time that I had the chance to see everyone at the wagon train following the incident with those horrid men. *The incident.* I'd nearly forgotten about it with the whirlwind of events that had transpired over the last few days. Would those horrible men be there? Would I have to face them at the meeting – their smelly bodies and their evil expressions? I decided that it was better to tell Mark now than for him to hear about it from anyone else. I attempted to explain it in the best way possible, but I could see his jaw firmly set, and his hands grip the reins tighter. It made me wonder at the wisdom of telling him at all.

We continued along in silence until we reached the thick, green pasture surrounding the lake where the wagons were assembled. The wagon belonging to those evil men was still parked a distance away from the others, just as it had been on that day. The wagon was quiet, and the men were nowhere to be seen. Were they nearby awaiting the meeting?

Mr. Wheeler, the wagon master, stepped out of his tent and waved as he caught sight of our buggy. His long stride quickly covered the distance between the tent and our buggy. Jeff and Thaddeus, his two younger trail hands, trailed along behind. Mark hopped down from the buggy, eager to greet them. It seemed that I had been temporarily forgotten.

"Mr. Peterson," I heard Mr. Wheeler say as he firmly shook Mark's hand. "I'm Benjamin Wheeler, the wagon master of this train. These are my two trail hands, Jeff and Thaddeus." He pointed to the young men, and they politely touched the rim of their hats. They must have discussed the fee because Mark dug into his pocket, counted out some bills, and passed them to Mr. Wheeler. The wagon master seemed pleased and shoved the bills deep into his pants pocket.

Bored from straining to listen and having been forgotten by my young groom, I scanned the uneven row of wagons until I spotted Claudia busy at work. I gathered the skirt of my dress in one hand and grasped the side of the buggy with the other, then hopped down and walked quickly toward her wagon. "Claudia!" I shouted and waved as I approached her family's camp.

"Yes?" She looked up from a large batch of dough she had been kneading at the table. "Why, Grace!" she exclaimed. "I didn't believe I'd ever lay eyes on you again! And don't you look the part of a prairie woman! I almost didn't recognize you!" She gave her mound of dough a firm pat and placed a white cotton tea towel over it. "Come sit down and tell me what's been going on with you these past few days. I'll just put on a pot of water for some tea, and we can visit while my bread's rising." She poured water from a bucket into a blue and white speckled teapot, then placed the pot in the glowing embers of a small fire she had going.

"Now sit down and tell me all about it!" She gave a weary, deep sigh, then plopped heavily down onto a bench and motioned for me to join her.

"Well, I'll be leaving with the wagon train when it leaves on Monday. I'm getting married tomorrow. My husband and I will be joining you." I waited for her shocked reaction, but she sat there smiling as I spoke. Apparently, it didn't seem to matter. "He's a pastor's son. I would like for you and your family to come to the wedding – if you can," I quickly added. Perhaps they didn't have proper clothes.

Claudia just continued to smile and nod her head. The teapot began to sing, sending faint cloud-like steam puffing out of the lip. She quickly walked to the fire, grasped the hot tea pot's handle with a thick towel, poured water into two blue metal cups, and then began dipping a tea strainer into the hot, steaming liquid. "Go on," she coaxed. "Did you find a wagon?" She handed me the first cup of tea and then began dipping the same tea leaves into her own cup. Mine was strong and bitter, but I didn't dare ask for sugar if she didn't offer.

"Yes, we did," I replied, "and a nice team of oxen as well." Not to be wasteful, I continued to sip on my tea and tried not to allow the bitter taste to show on my face.

"I just love hearing a good sermon!" Claudia exclaimed. "Will your husband be preachin' for us on the trip?" She sat the tea strainer down and began to sip on her clear, weak-looking tea. My heart was touched by Claudia's simple generosity: Although my tea was bitter and strong, she had given me the best of what she had.

I felt uneasy replying in Mark's stead about preaching. I was relieved when we were interrupted by him. "Grace, they're about ready to begin the meeting. Did you want to attend?" He gave Claudia a respectable nod.

"Yes, I certainly do! Mark, this is Claudia." I turned my attention back to my friend. "Were you planning to go?"

"No, I don't think so, Grace. You two go on ahead," she smiled warmly.

"Don't forget about the wedding tomorrow, if you can come. It's going to be right after Sunday morning services." I continued. "Afterward, there's going to be some food and cake at the Peterson's home. It'll be a good chance for the children to stock up on some sweets before we leave." I laughed and nodded toward the large group of children playing by the lake.

"Sure thing," Claudia smiled. "Like I said – noth'in I like better than good preachin, and the children would really like to have some good cake. It's hard to make that sort of thing on a campfire," she said. "Thank you for your invite. We will sure try to get there."

Mark took my arm, and we ambled away from Claudia's wagon – careful to avoid animal paddies hidden in the deep grass of the pasture.

"Have you preached any, Mark?" I asked out of curiosity.

"Not so far. I help with my father's ministry, but he does the preaching at church." We continued quietly together for a few more minutes. "What made you ask?"

"We'll talk about it later," I replied, quickly dismissing the matter.

Fourteen

Mr. Wheeler's Rules

Moreover, look for able men from all the people, men who fear God, who are trustworthy Exodus 18:21a

"We're going to be electing a Captain and Lieutenant to help keep order within the group," Mr. Wheeler stated as he eyed each of Monday's travelers attending the meeting. "And every man will be expected to take his turn keeping watch during the night. If anyone falls asleep during his watch, it could cost the entire group their lives. Understand?" The entire group nodded their heads simultaneously. "We're going to be heading into territory that could be hostile, so I'm going to lay out some strict rules here today. If everyone follows them, we might all get to the end of the trail safe and sound."

Mark and I exchanged serious glances during Mr. Wheeler's speech. I felt Mark's hand searching for mine, and I obliged him by moving mine closer. He found it and clasped my hand gently in his.

"One of the first rules is that we travel as a group." Mr. Wheeler's stern voice boomed. "If someone's wagon breaks down, everyone stops to help. If the wagon can't be repaired, we all divide up the load to help. If part of our party becomes ill, the entire group waits. If someone dies on the trail, we all help with the burial. We are traveling as a group," he emphasized once more. With furrowed eyebrows and a stern look, he examined the group for dissenters. "Anybody got a problem with that?" Everyone exchanged glances. No one spoke up.

"Widows and orphans. If anyone becomes widowed during the trip, all the men will pitch in to help the family and see to it that they arrive safely to our destination. Orphans will be found a new home as best as we possibly can. Any questions or comments?

Silence.

Don't shoot any game that you're not intending to eat. Be careful of your children. Children fall off the wagon seat and get run over, get snake bit, and break arms and legs all the time. There are no decent doctors on the trail until we reach a fort – only quacks with miracle medicines that don't help and cost a pretty penny."

"Men. Stay with the woman you brought. You know what I mean." Several of the men chuckled at this rule. Mr. Wheeler scowled at them. "You ever experience prairie justice? If you cause a problem or place the group in jeopardy, you'll see it real quick. And another thing – be careful with your gun. Out here it's for hunting game and protecting lives. Don't waste your ammo, or you'll be sorry you did. Every day we'll be up before sunrise to cook breakfast. While the women folk are cleaning up, the men will hitch their teams and get ready to move on. We'll make

Mr. Wheeler's Rules

a stop for lunch to eat and rest the animals; then, we'll cover as much territory as we can before sunset. Our goal will be to travel at least fifteen miles a day. Regardless, we'll go until I say stop. We must be across the mountains before winter sets in."

"Be sure to protect your money," he continued, "and bring plenty of it. The forts we'll stop at have blacksmiths and dry-goods stores. There are also rivers with ferry crossings. Some ferry owners are real bushwhackers and charge sixteen dollars for each wagon." This last comment set the group murmuring among themselves. Sixteen dollars was highway robbery!

"We will be leaving Monday morning right after breakfast. If you aren't here when we head out, we'll assume you changed your mind. We won't wait." He nodded in our direction, and everyone turned to look. I could feel my cheeks flush in embarrassment.

"Does anyone have leadership experience who would like to be considered for the position of Captain or Lieutenant?" Mr. Wheeler inquired.

A few men raised their hands, and our leadership election was underway. Each candidate was allowed to voice his experience, and with a show of hands, the men chose who would lead us. Once it was over, Amos Dixon, Claudia's husband, had been elected Captain, and Abraham White, Mary-Beth's father, was the Lieutenant of our little band of wagons.

***

Pastor Peterson's pleasant old mare trotted briskly down the soft, sandy road toward home. I was surprised when Mark continued straight down the road instead of making a right turn, which would take us to the Peterson's. He slowed the tired mare to a walk as we entered town and then halted her in front of the livery stable.

"Is something the matter?" I asked, concerned that the mare might have become lame.

"No," Mark reassured. "Nothing's wrong." He helped me out of the buggy and escorted me into the barn.

The barn was lined with stalls on either side – most of which were occupied, with a wide aisle that ran down the center. For a stable, it was fairly clean of horse droppings and boasted an ample pile of fresh yellow hay in each stall. The gentle black mare that I had rented a few days ago stood in the first stall, nibbling contentedly on sprigs of fresh hay and lazily swishing invading flies with her long, black tail. The elderly proprietor, a short frail-looking man with thinning gray hair, met us at the large barn doorway.

"Can I help you?" he inquired as he approached us.

"Perhaps," Mark responded casually. "We are going to be heading west this Monday. We have a team of oxen, but I may be interested in purchasing a horse if you have something that I like. Of course, it would have to be completely sound."

Mr. Wheeler's Rules

"Of course," the older gentleman repeated. "Do you see anything that interests you? If I do remember clearly, I believe this young lady rented this black mare a few days ago. What did you think of her?" I was no horse trader like Papa had been.

"She was nice," I said conservatively. From listening to Papa purchase horses, I knew that it was important not to act very excited about a horse you would like to buy. Otherwise, the price would go up!

"I could possibly let her go, that is . . . if the price were right," the gentleman said, looking very worried. Of course, his face said it all. She was the most valuable horse in the stable, and it would take a hefty sum to force him to part with her. But Mark was not to be swayed by the gentleman's performance.

"Well, we might wander around and look at the other horses before we leave," he told the proprietor. "There are several other horses for sale around Marshall. I could spend a lot of money, and the horse not even survive the trip." He pulled on my arm, and we casually strolled down the stable aisle, leaving the horse trader behind.

"Do you see anything that you like?" Mark asked. We stopped to look at a large chestnut with white socks.

"I'm not much of a horse expert," I admitted, "but I liked the black mare when I drove her out to meet Mr. Wheeler a few days ago. Of course, if she's too expensive . .

." I trailed off, worried that I may be suggesting too large an investment.

"We might get him to part with her for a decent price. Mr. Wheeler said that he and Jeff looked her over when they brought her back to the stable for you. He said that if he were in the market for a horse, he'd buy her himself. Said that she was so gentle you were able to handle her on your own. You know, it's always possible that you may finish this trip without me. That makes it important for you to be able to handle the animals by yourself if you need to." It was a grim thought, but I didn't protest because I knew that he was right. I may have to handle the animals myself.

We slowly strolled down the opposite side of the stable aisle looking at the other horses. The proprietor had disappeared, so we headed out to the buggy to leave. Mark assisted me up and began to climb into the seat alongside me when he reappeared from the barn. "Sir! Wait! Could I see you for a moment?

Mark gave me a discreet smile as he slowly climbed down from the seat. Both men disappeared into the barn's center aisle, leaving me to wait by myself.

"Hello, Miss!" I heard a man's shout from somewhere behind me. It was the sheriff ambling down the wooden sidewalk toward me. "Did things work out as you'd like?" He stopped at the side of the buggy and smiled.

Mr. Wheeler's Rules

"Yes, they certainly did, and I'll be heading west Monday morning after all." I couldn't help but smile as I said it.

"That's what I hear around town. I also heard that you will be getting married tomorrow." He leaned against the buggy to take a break from his rounds, gave a weary sigh, and adjusted the large gray hat on his head. "Not gossip," he assured, "just passing news. Not much goes on around here except when the wagon trains meet to head out in the spring. This is pretty much a church-going town. Your wedding with the pastor's son might be big news back east, but it's not unusual for a young couple to marry quickly and resettle here or somewhere else. I'll be in church tomorrow morning, so I'll be there for your wedding, too."

Just then, Mark came strolling out of the barn, proudly leading the black mare behind him. "Sheriff." Mark nodded respectfully. He led the mare to the buggy and securely tied her to the back.

The sheriff tipped his hat with a nod. "Mark. Miss. See you tomorrow in church," then resumed his afternoon rounds.

Mark carefully turned the pastor's mare around, and the four of us headed slowly for home. I turned sideways on the seat and watched our new mare amble casually behind the buggy. She had her ears tipped forward with a pleasant look about her as if she were smiling. Her long, black mane hung down across her neck like moss from an ancient oak.

She was black – coal black, except for a tiny white snip. It looked as if someone tapped her nose with a small paintbrush.

As we reached the cut-off road, Mark turned the buggy to the left toward home and clucked to the mare, urging her to pick up the pace to a slow jog.

We passed by Annie Mae's house just as she came running breathlessly out to the street, waving her arms wildly. "Mark! Grace! I think something terrible has happened. A man came by about an hour ago, looking for Rachel, Thomas, and the children. Said he was on a mission from the children's grandmother. Oh! I'm so afraid that she's changed her mind, and he came to take those children back. It would break Rachel's heart to lose them!" she moaned mournfully. "I didn't know what else to do! I told him where they were staying. I figured he'd find out anyway from someone else! I'm so sorry!" she wailed.

Mark's jaw firmly set as he looked toward home. "Miss Annie, you did the right thing," he reassured her kindly. "You're right; he would have found out, anyway."

He leaned forward in the buggy and slapped the long leather reins smartly against the mare's broad back. She raised her head quickly and jumped forward into an energetic canter. Our new black mare jumped forward, too, easily keeping up with the fast-moving buggy.

Mr. Wheeler's Rules

Miss Annie was right. As we pulled into the yard, there was a strange buggy and team waiting by the barn. Mark called out to a lanky young man with reddish-brown hair, who was ambling barefoot down the street carrying a fishing pole slung across his shoulder. "Joshua! Would you do me a favor?" Mark shouted urgently.

"Sure thing. What do you need?" The young man shifted his cane pole to the opposite shoulder and followed us into the Peterson's driveway.

"Will you cool these mares out and put them into stalls for me?

"Sure, Mr. Mark," he replied. He placed his long cane pole safely against the white, wooden fence of the Peterson's yard and spoke softly to the mares as he approached them.

Mark jumped down from the buggy and then quickly helped me down. We rushed across the yard and into the Peterson's home through the kitchen door. The entire family was sitting quietly in the parlor while little Emily amused herself with colorful wooden blocks on the parlor floor. Everyone's attention was focused on a tall, lanky man who sat on one of the kitchen's straight-back chairs facing them. Our abrupt entrance interrupted the meeting, and the startled group turned to stare at us.

Rachel handed Gabriel to Lydia and walked over to where we stood in the hall. She slid one of her arms around

Mark's back and one through my arm, gently guiding us into the parlor with the rest of the family.

"Mark, Grace, this is Mr. Williams. He is a neighbor of the children's grandmother, Lillie Newsome. He has come this morning to present a very generous offer that Mrs. Newsome has made to Thomas and me."

"Mr. Williams," Rachel stated, "this is my brother, Mark, and his bride, Grace. They're getting married tomorrow. They've been rushing about trying to get ready for their big event. Would you please continue about Mrs. Newsome's generous offer?"

Mr. Williams sat in the straight chair anxiously clasping his hat, which rested on his lap. "Like I was saying, Mrs. Newsome doesn't have any kin, and she's getting pretty well up in age. She doesn't have anyone to care for her, 'cept her neighbors. And she has her farm and the one next to it that her son owned. She said she misses them children something terrible, and her heart is broken all over again. Mrs. Newsome said that if you would move into her son's home, farm it, and help take care of her, she'll let you inherit both places when she passes on, just like her son would have. That way, she'll have family again, and her grandchildren will one day inherit what they have coming to them."

This time, it was Thomas' turn to speak. "Mr. Williams, it certainly is a generous offer that Mrs. Newsome has made . . . and it certainly was very neighborly of you to come all this way to present it. I think that if we were to move in, you both would make very good neighbors. I'm sure that you and Mrs. Newsome would understand if we took a little time to think about it. We have a small place of our own, and my folks won't be too excited if we move away, but it might be just the right thing to do, anyway. Would you please tell Mrs. Newsome that we will be by to see her later this afternoon after we've had a chance to discuss it?"

Mr. Williams nodded his head politely, stood, and thanked everyone for taking the time to listen to Mrs. Newsome's offer. Thomas escorted him to the door, then walked him out to his buggy.

"So?" Rachel asked. Her face was beaming. "What do you think?"

"You certainly would be closer to us than you are now," Mrs. Peterson stated excitedly, "and you would be well off financially." Little Emily climbed up onto her new grandmother's lap and received a warm hug.

Pastor Peterson joined in. "This reminds me of the Bible verse, 'The Lord is good to those who wait for him, to the soul that seeks him.'"

Thomas stepped back into the parlor, grabbed Rachel by the waist, and twirled around the room laughing. Little Emily laughed with them, and she was soon scooped up into her father's arms to join in the celebration.

I thought about the Bible verse that Pastor Peterson shared and how this sweet family had gone so quickly from being childless to having two precious children and an ample farmstead. I looked at my young, handsome groom who sat across the room and purposed in my heart that I would continuously seek the Lord's will as we set out on our long journey into the unknown.

Fifteen

Stepping Out in Faith

May the God of hope fill you with all joy and peace as you trust in him, so that you may overflow with hope by the power of the Holy Spirit. Romans 15:13

I sat listening to the small congregation sing from the pastor's study at the small clapboard church in Marshall. Hannah and Mrs. Peterson helped me to dress but were obliged to go to sit in the congregation to listen to the sermon. Pastor Peterson had promised he would not dawdle with the sermon, getting right to the point about needing a Savior and forgiveness of sins.

I looked at the beautiful array of flowers that Mark had picked for me this morning from Mrs. Peterson's flower garden. She'd woke him early and had the pastor shuffle him out of the house so that he would not see me before our wedding; but she had encouraged him to do one thing for me before he was banned from the house: gathering flowers for my bouquet. Although he didn't realize it, I watched him through a tiny opening in my bedroom curtains as he wandered around the garden, cutting flowers here and there. My bouquet was full of bright, fragrant spring flowers: the soft lavender of Wisteria, daintily flowing downward; the fragile petals of pink and white wild azaleas; the bright yellow and orange hues of daylilies. All of these and small sprigs of green lacy ivy were bundled tightly together and tied with a white, satin ribbon. It was not a bouquet that would have been found in an elaborate New York wedding, but it was elegant and sweet-smelling – a precious gift from my soon-to-be husband.

Michael, Mark's eldest brother, cracked the door open to the pastor's study. He was fashionably dressed in a dark suit – one which he said he used when he preached on special Sundays or performed weddings or funerals. His hair was slicked securely back, and he wore a pleasant, woody fragrance.

"Are you all right?" He casually stood in the wide doorway of the pastor's study.

"I think so," I responded nervously. "How do I look?"

For the first time, I felt quite unsure of myself. I slowly turned so that he could give a final inspection. I knew that the gown itself was beautiful. What did I look like to others, I wondered? Would Mark think that I was beautiful? The full-length mirror that Pastor Peterson used to inspect himself before Sunday services caught my attention once again. I was unable to keep from admiring the elegant gown which I wore. The tiny pearls, which were sewn into elaborate swirls on the gown's bodice, caught the late-morning streams of sunlight and sparkled brilliantly with blue and light purple hues. Soft folds of its elegant white satin material flowed generously down to the study's brightly polished floors. I had asked Hannah to braid my hair into one long braid down the back, and she had artistically woven tiny white flowers into it. The white, wide-brimmed hat and veil softened my face after having been exposed to much more sun the last few days than I was accustomed to.

I could see approval cross Michael's face and perhaps even a glimpse of affection. "You look very beautiful, Grace. Mark will be proud to have you on his arm. I will pray that things go well for both of you." His expression turned solemn, and he gave a thoughtful nod.

The sweet, soft music of the church's small pump organ drifted into us from the sanctuary. Michael held his elbow out for me to clasp. "I do believe that this is our cue," he said, smiling down at me.

We were both careful to keep from stepping on Mrs. Peterson's gown as we walked into the hallway that would lead us to the sanctuary. Jonathan stood at the large double doors, holding them closed until the proper moment. He smiled affectionately and gave me a brotherly wink as I stood, slightly trembling. I had a strange feeling, as if something were missing.

"My flowers!" I gasped in an increasing panic.

Michael quickly vaulted over the flowing train of his mother's wedding gown and raced into the study to retrieve the flowers. He appeared momentarily with my bouquet –

this time venturing around the gown's white train to resume his place by my side. With everything seemingly in place, Jonathan cracked the great doors enough to signal the church's organist with a nod. As he did, the organ music swelled, filling the entire church with its sweet, flowing rhapsody. Jonathan slowly opened the sanctuary's massive wooden doors.

I took a deep breath as I saw the tiny church crowded to capacity. The sheriff had attended, just as he said he would, although forced to stand in the corner because there were no more pews. Claudia, Amos, and their children were there, just as Claudia had promised. All seven small faces of the children were clean, and their hair was neatly combed into place. There was the small hotel clerk with his cowlicked hair. The mayor of Marshall was sitting in a pew with his beautiful wife and a row of neatly groomed little mayors beside them. Annie Mae was sitting on the aisle end of a pew. She was wearing a dark blue dress with small white dots on it. She had a white lace handkerchief that she dabbed her eyes with.

I spied Anita and Michael Collins from the wagon train group and their four cherubic little girls seated quietly beside them. Their row of blonde hair sparkled from the sun streaming in from a nearby window.

Abraham White, his lovely, shy daughter Mary-Beth, and his cold, stern-looking mother were there. Ben Wheeler, Jeff, and Thaddeus stood in the corner near the sheriff. Nita,

Jonathan's eldest daughter, sat primly on the aisle end of a pew. Her dress was light blue with narrow white stripes. Her sister Sarah was wiggling impatiently. Her thick, curly brown hair was already disheveled, and her new pink dress was wrinkled beyond hope.

Mrs. Peterson, dressed to perfection in a crisp, lavender frock with three-quarter sleeves, sat in the front row with the remaining Peterson family. Hannah sat next to her with her husband. Rachel and Thomas were next. Little Emily was restless in her father's lap, anxious to be allowed to toddle about. She tugged at her frilly blue and white gingham dress and swung her little legs impatiently back and forth. Sweet Gabriel was nearly asleep in his mother's arms. His little head, covered with soft, brown curls, was lying limply across Rachel's shoulder. Lydia sat at the end of the pew with Michael Junior, Mary, and Robert, next to her.

Mark looked handsome at the front of the church. He had a lovely white rose pinned to his dark suit. His thick blonde hair was neatly combed into place, giving him a boyish look. There was an awe-struck smile across his face as he watched me walk slowly down the aisle on the arm of his older brother.

Pastor Peterson, his thick grayish hair combed straight back and attired in a stately-looking dark suit, stood proudly beside him. His prayerful plan had come to pass. Somehow, through the grace of God, everything had fit together, nicely.

For such a small church, the trip down the aisle seemed unusually long. The sweet music stopped playing, and except for a few restless children, the entire congregation sat quietly.

"Who gives this woman away?" Pastor Peterson asked clearly so that his entire congregation could hear.

"I do!" Michael stated in a clear, sharp voice. He stepped aside and took his place beside Lydia.

What a bittersweet moment. It was a place that Papa should have filled – and yet, if Papa were still with me, I wouldn't have been standing there in that small clapboard church staring into the blue eyes of a man who had offered me an amazing adventure into the unknown with him.

Pastor Peterson made us exchange vows – pledging to love and honor each other throughout our lives until death claimed us. Perhaps, it was a promise that would be kept for just a short time. And then the time came for Mark to place the tiny gold band, which I had chosen myself, on my left third finger. It slid easily down to meet its companion, feeling cool against my nervous, clammy hand.

Mr. Peterson asked us all to bow our heads as he prayed fervently for our marriage, asking the Lord to help us grow spiritually together and to protect us on our long journey westward. Afterward, he pronounced us husband and wife, telling Mark that he could now kiss his bride.

Mark gently lifted the hat's white lacy veil from my face and fumbled briefly with it as he attempted to make it stay back. He gently placed his lips on mine, giving a proper church-like kiss, and then he gave a more passionate one – causing my heart to race wildly and my knees to grow weak. A few whistles and a hearty round of applause followed from the younger men of the congregation. I could only smile weakly in response. The organ's sweet music swelled to fill the crowded church. This time, it was my husband, Mark, who walked me slowly back down the aisle as we received everyone's best wishes.

Our very own gentle black mare had been hitched to Pastor Peterson's buggy. She stood patiently in front of the church, awaiting our departure. Everyone else had arrived separately in wagons to allow us our first ride together as husband and wife. The buggy was decorated gaily with paper flowers and streamers.

Mark gingerly helped me into the buggy, careful to tuck in the massive silk skirt of the gown as well. He bounded around the buggy to take his place beside me on the black leather seat and picked up the reins.

The well-wishers flowed out of the church and surrounded us. Mark expressed his appreciation. "Thank you everyone, for coming to such an important day for us! I understand that the best cooks in Marshall have prepared a wonderful wedding feast for us." Mark winked affectionately at his mother and laughed at the attention. "We're going home, and we look forward to seeing you there." He gave the mare a gentle flop of the reins across her backside, and we exited the church grounds under a generous shower of rice.

When we arrived at the Peterson's home, there was already a flurry of activity going on in and around the cottage. Some of the older church women of the Ladies Ministry, served the Lord by volunteering to help at special occasions. These faithful ladies made it possible for the pastor's wife to attend her son's wedding. The same wooden tables we'd used earlier were now festooned with tablecloths and vases of lovely wildflowers, and the wonderful aroma of food wafted out of the kitchen's screened door.

Mark drove our little mare to the barn, set the buggy's brake lever, and then bounded around to my side. He helped me pull the massive gown from around my feet and assisted me down.

Other buggies and wagons began to pull up to the house. One wagon held the young singles from the congregation. The occupants shouted joyously, hooted, and whistled – no doubt ready for a good time of fellowship.

The Peterson family arrived with Mrs. Peterson, anxious that everything go smoothly today. Her worries were all for naught because the women of the Ladies Ministry were already placing a variety of hot dishes and desserts on a long makeshift table. Pastor Peterson gave a short, thankful blessing, and our neighbors, friends, and family began the enjoyable task of filling their plates. Mrs. Peterson finally joined us but looked very ashen.

"Mama, what's wrong," Hannah asked.

"The icing flowers are missing from the cake, and there are small globs of icing missing . . ."

Hannah instantly had a scowl on her face. "Where's Sarah?" She stood abruptly from her chair, disappeared around the corner of the house, and returned shortly, carrying the little girl. Sarah was caught with the undisputable evidence: white cake icing in her hair, on her dress, and around her mouth.

Hannah carried the mischievous child to where Jonathan and Oneida were seated and plopped her down in a chair next to them. "Will you please keep track of your daughter?" She disappeared for a short time, then reappeared with a smile on her face. "The cake is fine now, Mama." She gave her mother's arm an affectionate squeeze.

As the feasting began to slow, two women from the Ladies Ministry carefully carried the wedding cake out and sat it on the table. It was decorated with sugared purple pansies and an ivy vine encircling the two lower layers of the cake. The cake's centerpiece was a small bouquet of sugared pansies tied with a silk ribbon. It was simple, but beautiful!

After everyone had their fill, Mark and I sat at a table and opened our wedding gifts. Some were simple but very necessary: needles, thimbles, thread, yarn, and knitting needles, along with jars of preserves and fruit. I opened one unusual gift that consisted of various colors and patterns of scrap material.

"I thought you might be needing a cradle quilt before you had enough scraps of your own," a simply dressed woman whispered into my ear. I thanked her sincerely, hoping that the blush from my embarrassment would go unnoticed.

I opened another present – this one from Lydia and Michael. It was a large brown bottle of horse liniment. "That'll come in handy," an elderly gentleman spoke up. "Your livestock may get pretty stiff from putting in so many miles a day," he continued.

Lydia slipped over to where we sat. "I thought you might be needing it," she explained quietly, "just in case you have to walk." I laughed softly and thanked her.

Pastor and Mrs. Peterson gave us a family Bible. It had a soft, brown leather cover and gold edges. I carefully flipped through the fragile pages and came to a section meant to record special events. Mrs. Peterson had thoughtfully recorded our wedding day: Marriage of Mark Peterson to Grace Ferrell.

With all the presents opened, we profusely thanked our guests. The white-bearded gentleman who had entertained us at the barbeque brought his fiddle out again and began to play. Just as they had at the first party, everyone formed a large circle and began to clap to the lively music – this time urging Mark and I to dance first.

It didn't take much encouragement to get Mark into the circle. He obligingly whooped loudly, grabbed me around the waist with one hand, clasped my hand with the other, and pulled me in with him. With my free hand, I quickly grabbed a handful of satin skirt to keep from tripping, and my husband took me on a whirling trip around the circle of wedding guests. Everyone joined in with us, keeping in step with the lively music of the fiddler. Thomas and two-year-old Emily whirled past us more than once during the evening. He let her sit on his arm and held her snugly with the other. Each time he whirled, she tipped her head backward and squealed with joy. Pastor and Mr. Peterson even joined in when the fiddler played a soft, romantic tune. I watched as they whispered and exchanged affectionate smiles. This would be how Mark and I would need to mold our own marriage if we were to be successful as well.

The party continued well into the evening. The Ladies Ministry had cleared and cleaned everything splendidly by the time the fiddler was too exhausted to continue. We exchanged many hugs and farewells to our guests and voiced our appreciation to those who had helped to make our wedding day special. By the time the last wagon pulled away, we were alone.

"That was fun, but now that everyone's gone, I'm exhausted," Mark stated. He wearily took my hand, and we strolled into the back of the house through the kitchen door. "My sisters prepared a surprise for us," he revealed. "Come with me." He led me to a guest room downstairs.

On the door was a beautiful wreath of ivy, white flowers, and satin ribbon. Mark slowly opened the door to a room softly lit with numerous white candles and festooned with lovely fragrant flowers and strewn petals. The sheets and quilt of the bed had been turned down. Mark put his finger to his lips for a moment when we could hear the soft conversation of his parents upstairs, then the click of their bedroom door as it closed.

He began to blow out the flame of each candle until there was only one remaining on the nightstand; then began to unbraid my hair, and gently ran his fingers through the length of it. His lips softly brushed my neck, and when the flame of the final candle was extinguished, my borrowed gown made a soft ssssshhhhhh as it cascaded to the floor.

***

Weary from the previous day, I awakened to Mark gently shaking me. "Grace, it's time to go." He placed my green calico dress on the bed, and I quickly threw it over my head and tied the sash.

We entered the kitchen into the arms of Mrs. Peterson. She tearfully made me promise to write and promised that she would keep us in prayer daily.

"Grace," she whispered, "We have been able to make it through very rough times because we have made Jesus the center of our lives. I promise that if you and Mark do, He will do the same for you. He will also see to it that you make your journey safe and sound. I know that He will," she emphasized.

Hannah hugged us next. "I have something for you." She brought out a book from under her shawl. "It's a journal. You can write about all the exciting adventures that you and Mark have on your journey. That way, next time you see us, you will be able to remember everything!"

Rachel hugged me tightly next. "We're going to be moving next to the children's grandmother. Now, we'll be close by when you write to Mama and Papa, so I can hear how you are doing!"

Quiet Oneida hung back from the group. When everyone else had finished their goodbyes, she stepped forward and placed a small box in my hands. "When you get down the road a bit, I imagine you will start to get hungry. I made some sandwiches for you and some of your wedding cake. It may be a while before you take your first break. I gave her a grateful hug and peeked into the box. Only smears of icing remained of the cake. Sarah stood behind her mother, intently focused on licking her fingers. Mark anxiously called my name, so I hurried to join him.

The Peterson women tearfully hugged Mark again and again. The men of the family, unsure of what to say at such an emotional moment, kept their hands in their pockets. Pastor Peterson openly dabbed a handkerchief at his eyes, wiping away the tears of a loving father. Mark helped me climb aboard the wagon and picked up his driving pole.

"I guess this is it," he announced, unsure of what to say next. I could tell he was hesitant to leave and anxious to meet with the others at the same time. Pastor Peterson decided for us.

"Let's all bow our heads together, one last time as a family, and ask the Lord to guide and protect Mark and Grace on their journey."

We all obediently bowed our heads as the pastor began to speak to the Lord on our behalf. Soft, gentle sobbing filled the background of his deep, somber voice.

"Son, it's time for you to go," he said finally, with quiet authority. Mark firmly shook his father's hand, then gave him one last hug. He quickly climbed aboard our wagon and shrilly whistled to our team of oxen. They obediently leaned into their yoke and slowly began to move us out of the Peterson's yard. Our little black mare neighed a farewell to the pastor's mare. She followed slowly along behind, tethered to the wagon.

"Wait a minute! Wait a minute!" a familiar voice broke through the emotional exit as Annie Mae drove her buggy quickly into the Peterson's yard. "Mercy sakes alive! I thought that I was going to miss you!" she shouted. "Grace, I want you to have this here rocking chair. Lord knows He might just call me home anytime now – and I would rather know that you could put it to good use! Mark looks healthy," she stated brashly, "you may need it sooner than you think!" Everyone laughed at her usual bluntness. The men quickly tied it securely to the back of the wagon for us. We sincerely thanked her, but needing to make good time, Mark whistled again to the oxen team. Everyone stood in the dirt road behind us, waving until we were well out of sight.

I looked at the man sitting next to me, my new husband. His strong jaw was set in determination, and his clear blue eyes focused on the destiny that lay before us. I felt safe and loved by this man of God whose very smile now made my heart flutter. I sighed contentedly, scooted closer, and rested my head on his strong shoulder.

Papa was right. My dowery did provide a new life for me. Not in a grand way in a fine house with Jerrold as he would have imagined, but in a square box, pulled by two brown oxen, with a husband I hardly knew.

The series continues with ***On Destiny's Trail***

ABOUT THE AUTHOR

The Author, Phyllis Godwin, and her husband, Harry, serve as Chaplains for Cowboys for Christ, sharing the Good News of the Gospel of Jesus Christ. They've been married for over 42 years and have 4 children. Cowboys for Christ is a non-denominational Christian organization serving the livestock and equestrian communities.

Made in the USA
Columbia, SC
27 April 2025